Widow's Wake

Volume 3 of The Sisters' Saga

Alison Ferguson

Backstory Press

For Ian

Contents

Chapter 1

This is the only way

Henrietta

Henrietta wove her way through the press of the crowd on the wharf bidding their farewells. She scanned the faces, in search of Griffith, stopping only when the importunate claimed an acquaintance. But then she moved on as quickly as she could. Without her brother's help, she faced a grey future.

She stiffened her back—she might be forty-seven but she wasn't ready to give up yet. Admittedly, her black widow's dress was sombre, but it gave her figure an alluring definition. The eyes of the gentlemen followed her movements discreetly while they ostensibly talked and laughed and exchanged messages to be passed on when the ship arrived in England.

Above the heads and shoulders of the jostling throng, Henrietta saw a small feminine hand waving from the crowd of passengers waiting to board. Mrs McPhail was still puffing from her exertions when Henrietta reached her.

'Well, we're here at last. We've only just arrived by carriage, though why we didn't come yesterday, I don't know, it would have been much simpler. Young Joseph and Bridget seemed to think it would work out fine, but here we are, late.'

Henrietta nodded to acknowledge Miss Bridget McPhail standing by her brother's side and surrounded by their farewelling friends.

'We are in plenty of time, Mama. See, the captain hasn't even begun to call off the passenger list,' Miss McPhail said with a smile, one hand raised to cover her crooked teeth.

'All very well, but we need to check that our baggage has got on board. I told you we should have brought a servant with us for the voyage but, as usual, I was overruled. You two will need to attend to it. Off you go.'

A couple of the gentlemen promptly disengaged from their group of friends and began to forge a path for Miss McPhail and Joseph between the barrow boys and laden carts.

Mrs McPhail gazed after them and whispered to Henrietta, 'That tall one on the left. He's the one who got away.' She shook her head ruefully. 'Such a lovely young man, so attentive, but it seems he has taken a fancy to one of Bridget's friends, and so there's nothing to be done about it.'

Henrietta smiled. 'Sydney is a small pond, Mrs McPhail, and London will offer a much larger pool—a veritable angler's paradise, so I'm told.'

Mrs McPhail sighed, perhaps estimating the possibilities and coming up short.

Taking advantage of the pause, Henrietta said, 'Is that Alfred Ferris I can see? Please excuse me, Mrs McPhail. I must ask him to pass on my goodbyes to Lady Ferris.'

If anyone knew what was keeping Griffith, it would be Alfred Ferris.

Alfred stood among the people gathered by the carriages and horses, with another young man. Like many men who found themselves balding at a young age, the man talking with Alfred had compensated by cultivating a large amount of facial hair. His bushy moustache was familiar, but the name wouldn't come.

She slowed her pace, searching her memory. Her son Arthur had spent a lot of time in his company before he had left for London. The young man was connected to Lady Ferris somehow. She nearly had it—he had worked on the Ferris' property up north. One of Lady Ferris' nephews, his father had been a plantation owner in Jamaica. But she'd reached them and still his name eluded her.

'We've been hearing all about Mayhew's property down near Yass,' said Alfred by way of greeting.

Henrietta didn't know if he'd sensed her panic or whether he had said the name by chance—but for whichever it was, she was grateful—Mr Morgan Mayhew.

'In Yass? I had in mind that you were still up north, Mr Mayhew?' she asked.

'You are most kind to remember, Lady Wood.'

'I was just saying to Mayhew,' said Alfred, 'that I don't envy you the journey, given the company, what with pompous old Berkeley for conversation.'

Henrietta tried to keep her face impassive as Mr Mayhew laughingly moved on to make his farewells to his other friends.

Alfred drew her aside. 'Griffith is on his way with the items you're to take with you. My best wishes for the outcome of your mission, Lady Wood. My mother is so very appreciative that you have taken it on.'

Henrietta was startled. 'Lady Ferris? She doesn't know of the … items, surely?'

'No, no, of course not. Only about the petition for the full pensions. If you are successful, then you both will be able to live in the manner that you deserve.'

Henrietta took her time returning to the gangway, where her maidservant waited, guarding their last pieces of hand luggage. Overhead, the gulls shrieked and wheeled about the baskets of fish being hauled across from the neighbouring vessel. She drew in the salty air infused with the rich animal smells of wool and hide being loaded into the hold for the journey to London.

Now that she knew Griffith was on his way, she permitted herself to mentally berate him for being so late. Her mission to gain the full pension depended on her having something to bargain with. She would be asked to board any minute, and he still wasn't here. At this rate, she might only be able to wave to him from the rail and then where would she be?

'Are the parrots' cages well positioned, Hill?' she asked her maidservant, trying to distract herself.

'Not the best spot, I'm afraid, milady. Someone had bolted their own cages there, so I couldn't move yours, but I got 'em high up off the ground. Dunno if that'll keep the rats off but …'

Henrietta tapped her feet in irritation.

Captain Gallagher stood by the gangway, greeting the passengers. 'Lady Wood, an honour to have you with us,' he said.

'I look forward to it,' she replied. Nearly ten years had passed since Mr Justice Wood had been elevated to the position as Chief Justice and awarded a knighthood, but Henrietta never tired of being called 'Lady Wood'.

'You've no need to be worrying about the trip in a sound ship like the *Lord Henderson*,' the captain continued.

'My thanks, Captain Gallagher. I'm sure the voyage will be at least as pleasant as the five I have previously taken.'

The captain turned abruptly to the second mate. 'Mr Nash, time to be getting this lot on board.'

'Lady Wood?' asked Mr Nash.

Henrietta tried to hide her vexation. No doubt he meant to observe the courtesies of rank, but she wanted anything but to board first.

'If I may, Mr Nash, I would prefer to delay boarding a little longer.'

Captain Gallagher spoke over him. 'I'm sure that as an experienced traveller you will understand that time and tide wait for no man or, in this case, woman, Lady Wood.'

Before she could reply, the captain's attention was taken by the arrival of the first mate. The two men drew aside, conversing in low tense voices.

'Mr Jackson tells me the pilot is making trouble,' the captain barked at Mr Nash. 'Since Mr Jackson doesn't seem able to deal with it by himself, I'll leave you to finish up here.'

Mr Nash exchanged a look with Mr Jackson and then returned to his list.

'Hill, you go on ahead with my bits and pieces. Please, Mr Nash, do proceed with the other passengers.'

Mr Nash, nonplussed for a moment, nodded and moved on to the Berkeleys and their clutch of children.

Henrietta searched again for any sign of Griffith, increasingly annoyed. When the two of them sailed to Calcutta as adolescents without their parents, it had been the same story. At every port along the way, she'd been the one waiting for Griffith to get back on board while the captain fretted about losing one of his charges. For a man who'd spent most of his career on a ship, Griffith was remarkably cavalier about keeping to time. And to be late when it really mattered …

It was easy to keep watching Mr Nash, a strikingly handsome and well-built young man. There were a lot of good-looking young men about, now that she took the time to look. Or was it that as she got older, all young people appeared handsome, simply because of their youth? Mr Mayhew was standing with a number of young gentlemen and a few men from the regiments stationed in Sydney. From what she could hear, a couple of them would be fellow passengers.

'Cheer up, Gordon,' said one of the soldiers to a fellow lieutenant from the 99th, decked out in his red regimental coat. 'From what I've seen so far, the voyage looks set to let you concentrate on making up your losses from last night's cards. No delightful young ladies to tempt you from bachelorhood on this trip, unlike some other trips I could mention.'

'I thought you were telling us that you are bent on finding a wife in London,' said another. 'You need to start as you mean to finish. I see from the list that there's a young Miss McPhail who will be on board.'

'Only partly right,' said his friend. 'Miss McPhail is listed as a passenger, but young is not the description I would have chosen.'

'Well you know what they say ...' another began, but the group moved towards the end of the gangway and their voices were lost in the hubbub.

The crowd around Henrietta had thinned out and the only people nearby were a tall, thin man with his wife. Their servant was holding their child. The wife's face was drawn, her eyes sunken.

'Mr and Mrs Veitch,' called Mr Nash.

The man took his wife's arm in a tight grip— Henrietta could see his wife wince. After a moment, like a statue breaking, she took a step forward and he began to propel her towards the ship.

Henrietta was so focused on the couple that she had stopped looking about for her brother. She searched the crowd one last time.

There—there he was—waving from the line of carriages.

'Lady Wood.' Mr Nash approached her. 'You're the last left on my list. Are you ready to board, milady?'

'Mr Nash, thank you so much for indulging me. May I trouble you a little further? I've just seen my dear brother.'

Mr Nash's dazzling white teeth smiled down at her. 'Between you and me, Lady Wood, I think the problem with the pilot will take a bit of sorting out.'

Henrietta weaved her way through the throng with quick steps and then leapt lightly up the stairs to the pavement.

'Steady on,' said Griffith laughing. 'They're not going to leave without you.'

'I wouldn't be so sure about that. Captain Gallagher does not appear to be a man easily budged.'

'In that case, you clearly haven't had enough time to work your charm on him. He'll be eating out of your hand by the time you reach London.'

'And here you are, trying to charm me out of being cross with you for being so late.' She affectionately straightened his neckerchief, which was askew—as usual. 'You know, Eliza has long gone back home, and all your nephews and nieces were most vexed to have missed their favourite uncle.'

'I'll be seeing your daughter and her brood soon enough.' While he was talking, he drew a small packet from inside his coat. 'Are you sure about this? It's dangerous and there's a long way to go. Besides, what you're spending would keep us for a year, if we were careful.'

What if Griffith were right and it all proved to be a waste of time and money? She would be back here— back to life as a poor widow, having to account for every penny spent. Fighting back the bile, she remembered the enforced gratitude of dependency. Perhaps the whole journey would be for naught.

'We've been through this. Besides, we're neither of us very frugal, are we? This is the only way. If I can only speak with Lord Grey.' Her tone dropped to its most persuasive. 'Like Papa did with Lord Liverpool, you know, back when he was so angry about Bligh. Governor Gipps did promise, didn't he?'

'Apparently, Lord Grey owes Gipps. So yes, as soon as Grey agrees, Gipps has given his word to push it through the Legislative Council.'

Satisfied, Henrietta took the packet and tucked it into her reticule. 'Do you know what's inside?' she asked.

Griffith scanned the crowd to ensure they couldn't be overheard. 'I'm not about to break the seal on secret documents, now am I? But I do know that they'll expose the revolutionaries working to bring down the new French monarchy. Lord Grey will be more than willing to reward your service. But, there's a problem …'

'What?'

'This is only half of them. They divided them into two packets, for better security. I picked this packet up when I sailed through the Friendly Isles, but the second lot haven't arrived yet.'

Henrietta couldn't believe he had waited until now to tell her. 'Then is this packet still worth anything?'

'Yes, yes, it must be,' he said, avoiding her eye.

Henrietta knew her brother too well. Without the complete set of documents, the information would be worthless—otherwise, why split them?

'You see, Alfred says he expects the second lot to get here any day,' Griffith added. 'If we can get them on the next ship headed to London, why then you'll have them. You might even get hold of them before you even arrive, if I can find a faster ship than the *Lord Henderson*.'

She shook her head. So much was uncertain.

The ship's bell sounded. Griffith took her arm and they walked down to the ship together in silence.

'Boarding now, milady?' Mr Nash said hopefully.

Clustered by the base of the gangway, the soldiers were still calling their last farewells to their comrade.

'Hoy, Gordon,' one shouted up to him. 'Don't forget to count your cards!'

Griffith's head jerked around at the mention of the name. His face greyed as he spotted Lieutenant Gordon by the rail.

'Not Gordon,' he groaned, under his breath. 'Oh, Henrietta, what have I done?' He grasped both her hands tightly. 'Don't let him get an inkling of what you're up to, you hear? And, be careful.'

'Lady Wood?' Nash asked again, his voice plaintive.

'But Griff—?'

Nash began to herd Henrietta up the gangway.

Griffith called after her, 'Promise me you won't get desperate and catch the eye of some rich merchant in London and do anything foolish. You will come back, won't you?'

Chapter 2

She cast her eye over the gentlemen on deck

Henrietta

Griffith's reaction on seeing Lieutenant Gordon shook Henrietta so much that she stayed by the rail staring back after him. The ship was undertow, and she tried to slow her heart to the steady chug of the steamer dragging them away from the docks. Was Griffith warning her the lieutenant knew about the packet of documents? Would Lieutenant Gordon be prepared to get them from her in any way he could?

By the time the ship anchored in Watsons Bay to wait for the pilot, Henrietta told herself not to be so melodramatic. Lieutenant Gordon was probably a known womaniser, and Griffith was simply warning her not to fall for his charms. Perhaps he thought she would confide in him about the documents. By late afternoon as dinner was served, she was angry with Griffith for thinking of such a thing. She might indulge in the occasional flirtation, but she'd never betray their secret. It was far too important.

The cuddy, a well-appointed cabin at the stern, was cramped and noisy, with the number of children greatly adding to the bedlam. Three times Mr Quigley attempted to sip the soup only to have his spoon jolted out of his grip.

'This won't do, it won't do at all,' he grumbled to Mr Veitch.

'I am so sorry, Mr Quigley,' Mrs Berkeley said, removing one of the twins from where he had started drawing circles with his finger in the spilled soup on the table. 'The chief steward has promised there will be an earlier sitting for the children's dinner once we're under way.'

On the other side of the table, Mr Dempster tried to engage Miss McPhail in conversation. 'I understand this is your first trip?' he asked.

'Yes, I'm not much of a sailor, I'm afraid,' Miss McPhail replied, seemingly without much interest.

'So, you've had some experience, by the sound of it,' Mr Dempster tried again.

'I'm so glad we've been able to enjoy our dinner in the calm of the harbour at least,' Miss McPhail said, this time directing her comment at Lieutenant Gordon, who had loaded his plate with a small mountain of food.

'Last time I was on the 'arbour,' cut in Mr Owens, his mouth full, 'I was as sick as a cat.'

'Language, Mr Owens,' his wife said, looking in Henrietta's general direction.

'Sailing in the harbour is an admirable sport,' said Mr Dempster in a transparent bid to regain Miss McPhail's attention. 'Only the other day I was out with Mr Blake on his yacht—'

'Clearly the legal business is doing well for him,' said Mr Mayhew. 'I caught sight of him on the *Sylph* as we were towed across from Sydney Cove. Doesn't the man do any work?'

'Might I enquire if you play cards, Lady Wood?' Mr Akers, the ship's surgeon, was seated to Henrietta's left. Somehow, he'd ended up with the Veitch's four-year-old on his lap, as Mrs Veitch had pleaded a headache and stayed below in her cabin. Mr Veitch was ignoring his son.

'Yes, indeed, I always find cards a profitable way to pass the time on a long voyage,' she said.

'Profitable, in more ways than one, I'm hoping,' Lieutenant Gordon muttered to Mr Mayhew.

There was a bustle of commotion over by the door as young Charley Berkeley staggered into his sister, Adelaide. He'd been leaning against the door when someone tried to open it from outside. All heads turned to see Captain Gallagher.

'Lieutenant Gordon,' said the captain. 'This gentleman is Mr Brown, a bailiff.' He moved to one side, revealing a bulky man towering behind him.

Mr Brown stepped forward and laid his hand on the lieutenant's shoulder. Lieutenant Gordon's weather-worn face paled under its tan and he made a move to rise, but Mr Brown's heavy hand pinned him to his seat.

'I'm arresting you at the suit of Mr Bow, innkeeper at the Moreton Bay, for the sum of £49.' He grasped the lieutenant by the arm and pulled him to his feet.

Even the children were quiet as Lieutenant Gordon, stony-faced, was frog-marched out in the company of the bailiff and the captain. Then everyone spoke at once.

'Well, I never,' Mr Sapsford spluttered.

'To think, we were harbouring a fugitive from justice,' said Mrs McPhail, her voice tinged with excitement.

'Good thing they got him before we'd left.' Mrs Sapsford adopted a smug expression.

'Of course, the charges may well be unfounded,' intoned Mr Berkeley slowly.

Henrietta saw Mr Mayhew and Mr Dempster exchange a meaning-laded glance. They at least seemed to have expected it. Was it a coincidence, she wondered, or had Griffith set the bailiffs on him? She doubted he had the kind of money to settle his debts.

'Even if the matter can be settled, he'd be fortunate to make it by road there and back and be on board before we sail,' she offered, smiling happily.

Mr Akers nodded. 'The *Cornubia* should be back within the hour to tow us out of the Heads. He hasn't a chance.'

With the meal finished, the passengers began to drift from the cuddy, many declaring their intention to ready themselves for their first night at sea. Those with children were aiming to get them in bed, in the vain hope they'd fall asleep before they got into open water.

Mr Dempster followed the McPhails out into the passageway. 'Do let me know if you need any assistance with moving your luggage about or anything,' he said to Mrs McPhail. 'I know it can be trying to travel without a servant.'

'My thanks, Mr Dempster,' she replied stiffly. 'But I'm sure my decision to leave our servants to take care of the house was sensible. One of the stewards will be able to attend to our needs satisfactorily.'

'And I'm here to help,' young Joseph McPhail spoke up, his voice cracking in its attempt to sound manly.

'Of course,' said Mr Dempster. 'But I mean, don't hesitate to ask.'

Having shed the weight of her worries about Lieutenant Gordon, Henrietta made her way to the main deck, along with others keen to watch as they passed through the Heads. She collected her woollen shawl on the way—the early evening air at this time of year would carry a hint of autumn.

As she expected, Mrs Berkeley had stayed in the cabin with the children, but Henrietta joined Mr Berkeley by the rail. Mr Owens stood nearby looking across to Middle Head. Mrs Sapsford made rather a show of situating herself on the side of Mr Berkeley away from Mr Owens.

'How are the children settling, Mrs Sapsford?' Henrietta asked.

'They'll be fine—they're all good sailors, and Mabel will have them sorted out in a trice.' She paused and added, 'It was kind of you to ask.'

'There she is,' Mr Owens called out, pointing to the little steamer heading in their direction. 'Wunnerful thing, steam, innit?' He sighed in satisfaction, watching the *Cornubia* as it came back alongside.

'Indeed it is,' said Mr Berkeley. 'I have read that within five years we'll be travelling all the way to London by steamer.'

'Is that the *Cornubia* back?' Mrs McPhail squeezed in by the rail next to Henrietta. 'Bridget and I decided we couldn't be bothered sorting out everything in the cabin. We've got a whole four months to do that.'

They watched as the pilot boarded. Both Captain Gallagher and the first mate met him. Their voices were raised enough that fragments could be caught by the passengers.

'We made an agreement, Mr Jackson. Ten shillings is what you agreed to, and I'll not be paying more.'

Mr Jackson set his legs apart as if to emphasise his words. 'I'm standin' my ground. When I contracted with Mr Jackson 'ere,' he said, indicating the first mate, ''e told me the *Cornubia* would be coming back into the 'arbour and so could bring me back once she's towed you outside. Then today 'e tries to tell me the *Cornubia* is 'eading on up the coast. So I've got to 'aul my boat along wiv us, and pay the crew for the rowin' back in. So that'll cost yous extra. That's all I'm sayin'.'

The men continued their dispute as they walked out of earshot.

The *Cornubia* blew her whistle and she pulled away, untethered to the *Lord Henderson*.

'Looks like we might not be leaving tonight, after all,' said Mr Dempster, who'd come up on deck during the argument. Henrietta saw that Mr Akers had also emerged.

'We'll be stuck here for days if they can't sort it out,' said Mr Sapsford.

They watched the approach of the captain with apprehension. Mr Jackson had been left to continue the negotiations with the pilot.

'My apologies, ladies and gentlemen, our departure has been unavoidably delayed. Circumstances beyond our control.' He shot a dark look to where the pilot and

Mr Jackson were lowering the jolly-boat to row Mr Jackson back to the pilot station at Watsons Bay.

'Well I, for one, am grateful,' said Mrs McPhail. 'That's at least one more night when I'll be able to get a good night's rest.'

'So, captain,' said Mr Dempster, 'this may be the first of many delays. When do you think we'll reach England? How about a wager?'

'The *Lord Henderson* is the fastest ship afloat for her size, but I never bet on the weather, Mr Dempster,' said the captain.

'I'll take you on,' said Mr Akers, drawing out a notebook. 'Best to keep a record of wagers won and lost, I always think. I'll wager she'll get us to London before a hundred days are out.'

'So when does that get us there?' asked Mrs McPhail, her eyes screwed up with the effort of the calculation. 'If we leave Port Jackson tomorrow, and there are thirty days in May, so—'

'A hundred days will get us in by Saturday, 12th of June,' said Mr Akers as he wrote it down. 'So how much are you putting on this, Mr Dempster?'

'How does ten shillings sound?'

'Done,' Mr Akers said with a flourish of his pencil.

When Henrietta returned to her cabin, she was relieved to see that Hill had put it to rights. Now she could decide where to secrete the packet of documents. Part of the complexity of travel was the ordering and retrieval of the necessarily restricted number of things you could take with you. Once unpacked, the selection could be enjoyed for its simplicity. By the end of the voyage, she knew she would have come to loathe the much worn and used items and would be hungering for novelty—but even such a craving would have its delights as she reclaimed, like long lost treasures, the things stowed away for arrival. This made for a difficult problem as to where to locate the documents where neither Hill nor a visitor would inadvertently notice them.

Her cabin was the largest on board and, although she had decided not to bring her piano this voyage, she had brought with her a number of books and a small writing desk. Perhaps this was the trip during which she would finally get around to writing her memoir. Everyone she knew who had heard her stories of the colony in its early days and her time in India urged her to do so. But there never seemed enough time—and besides, forty-seven wasn't old enough to be penning her biography.

With almost any other servant, she could have put the documents in the writing desk, but Hill had learnt to read as well as sew as a child at the Female Orphan School in Parramatta. Perhaps she could hide them among her art materials?

'Milady,' Hill said, brushing Henrietta's hair out. 'James, the assistant steward, he says the lieutenant from the 99th got taken off by the bailiff while you was all having your dinner.'

'Yes, it was embarrassing for everyone concerned. I would have thought the captain could have arranged for the arrest to be managed more discretely.'

Thinking back, Henrietta realised she hadn't been the only one of the company who'd been pleased by Lieutenant Gordon's departure. Mr Dempster had positively beamed. Given his attentions to Miss McPhail throughout dinner, perhaps he thought of Gordon as a rival. Though—Miss McPhail's blushing face came to mind—she had barely raised her eyes from her plate, except to gaze after Gordon as he was manhandled out of the room.

'You was back earlier than I expected.' Hill coiled Henrietta's hair into a loose plait. 'I'd only just managed to get your bunk made up. I needed James to give me a hand, the mattress is that heavy. I thought, what with the delay and all, that you'd all be playing cards for hours yet.'

'No takers tonight, Hill. A dull evening all round, if we don't count the lieutenant's misfortune.' She cast a glance to the trunk where she'd stowed her meagre funds. If the size of tonight's wager was anything to go by, the stakes of card games for this voyage were likely to be high. She'd better hope fortune was smiling on her.

After Hill had left, she retrieved her mahogany painter's box and inserted the packet underneath the top tray, with her oil rag acting as a shield against prying eyes. That done, she felt calmer. There was only one more problem. How would the rest of the documents reach her? *Well, that's out of my hands, so I need not worry,* she told herself.

Henrietta rose early hoping to be on deck as the ship passed out of the Heads. She drew her shawl tight around her. The chill breeze was so light that the sailors fought to catch it as Mr Jackson fumed under the captain's censorious eye.

She hadn't slept well, unable to push the second packet of documents from her mind. If it were to be delivered to her in London, then that would be fine. Why couldn't that be the plan? She didn't understand why Griffith had placed such stress on the fact that a following ship might catch up with the *Lord Henderson,* and then she could get hold of the documents earlier. If by some lucky chance the two ships did cross paths and by an even luckier chance pass along mail, then she supposed the documents might be disguised as a parcel for her, but that was surely a great risk. And what if someone, a sailor perhaps, on the following ship were to attempt to transfer the documents in some other way?

An ally, that's what she needed. She cast her eye over the gentlemen on deck. Mr Owens was smoking his morning pipe up on the poop, talking with Mr Mayhew who gave her a wave in greeting. Trusting Mr

Owens was out of the question. She couldn't imagine so much as a conversation with him. She considered Mr Mayhew as he came down from the poop.

He struck her as handsome, though nothing remarkable—in this, he reminded her of her first husband, poor, useless Patrick Richeley. Mr Mayhew's bearing and demeanour were mature, but even at twenty-eight, his open countenance persisted. She suspected it would still be as easy to slip beneath the veneer as it had been when her son Arthur befriended him on his arrival in the colony when he was twenty. She had no doubt she could get him to do anything she asked—but keep a secret? No, his was no poker face.

'So, Mr Mayhew, I understand you are heading home to be married?' she asked.

'Aunt Clara told you, I suppose.'

'Yes, Lady Ferris is quite vexed with you. She says you will not tell her who is to be your bride. It has all been a mystery indeed. And Arthur wrote to me from London that he'd heard rumours and he's told me to find out all about it.'

Mr Mayhew fingered his moustache, smoothing the hairs outward from the centre with his thumb and forefinger, but stayed silent.

'You have had us thinking there was something wrong with the young lady. Lady Ferris and I have come up with the most frightening conjectures. Your bride cannot be tainted with the stain of convict parents, or else you would not need to return home to

England to marry her. Perhaps, her parents have forbidden the match and you intend to elope? That would, of course, be—'

'No, no, nothing of the sort,' interrupted Mr Mayhew, tetchily. 'I've become almost superstitious about telling anybody at all. I had to delay my plans to leave so many times I began to wonder if it ever would occur. I will write to Aunt Clara at the earliest opportunity now that things are underway.'

Henrietta felt like giving him a shake. 'And the bride is …?'

'My cousin,' he said tersely.

Henrietta searched her memory. Lady Ferris often talked about her family, but Henrietta tended to find her mind wandered when it came to cousins she had not met.

Then it came to her.

'Young Amelia Butler, how lovely—my congratulations to you …' Her voice tailed off when she saw the horror on his face.

'No, no, of course not, Amelia was a child of nine when I left. No, I am engaged to her older sister, Miss Lucy Butler. We've known each other since Aunt Agnes brought the family to live with us in Gloucester after her husband died.'

'She has waited a long time if you have been away, what, for over five years?'

'Seven.'

'That is certainly a long time. I'm sure I could not wait so long.' She laughed, thinking of her first marriage at fifteen. She and Patrick had thought three months was far too long to wait and had pestered Uncle Piggott until he had relented, perhaps concerned about the risks of delay to her virtue. 'There are so many temptations for young people, aren't there?' she said.

Mr Mayhew's eyes widened at her implication.

'I mean no disrespect to your cousin, of course. But a handsome young man like yourself, why, even on this ship there is Miss McPhail, with all her accomplishments, as I'm sure her mother will tell you.'

Mr Mayhew frowned. 'Miss McPhail is, indeed, an accomplished lady. Mr Dempster tells me she beat him at chess last night,' he said.

'Is Mr Dempster such a master of chess then? You sound shocked. So, you cannot be tempted by intelligence in a prospective wife?'

Mr Mayhew ignored her. 'Seven years is not so long as to expect substantial changes at home,' he answered.

'Well, I am sure you will find everything as you remember it. For my part, I am not as sure. I was but a child of six when Sir Joseph Banks convinced my father that what the colony needed were the Burbridge brothers—' She broke off her story, looking up at the sails hanging limp.

'Oh, no—at this rate, we'll be lucky to get out the Heads today.' Mr Mayhew paced about. 'What was the problem with last night anyway?'

'Don't you know? The pilot wanted to be paid more, but the captain wouldn't have any of it.'

'I was down in the hold to check on my budgerigars. Some blighter had moved his cages up to where mine had been. The poor things were shivering down on the floor, surrounded by water, from who knows where.'

'Morning all. Why aren't we moving?'

When Henrietta turned, her breath caught in her throat.

It was Lieutenant Gordon. His regimental coat had been slept in and hung open. The stubble on his chin and generally unwashed appearance suggested a hard night.

'I see you were able to join us, Lieutenant Gordon,' said Henrietta, trying to sound calm. 'I had thought we might not have your company for the voyage.'

'It is indeed only by luck I managed to be here, Lady Wood.' He gave a wry smile. 'Or rather, the luck that Mr Blake has to sail the harbour for sport. Mr Brown knew him of course, and he gave him a hoy and he conveyed us into Sydney.'

'So you could settle the matter?' asked Mr Mayhew, sounding surprised. 'Manning told me that you—'

Lieutenant Gordon cut him off. 'It was a narrow thing, but I spotted McKenzie out of the window of the room where Mr Brown had me incarcerated. He answered my calls, and like the fine fellow he is, he paid the surety for me.'

'A generous friend indeed,' said Henrietta, tight-lipped.

Lieutenant Gordon shrugged. 'Well, I've forgiven him a few losses to me at cards over the last couple of years. McKenzie said the ship was delayed, so here I am, and very glad to be so.'

Was it her imagination or was he looking at her meaningfully when he said this? *Well, I refuse to be intimidated*, she thought. *There's nothing I can do about his presence, so I'll simply have as little to do with him as I can.* Still, she reflected, she wasn't going to be the only one troubled by his return—Mr Dempster might share some of her disappointment, although for different reasons.

Lieutenant Gordon was without a doubt the only person on board who was cheerful about the delay. As the morning became afternoon, without sufficient breeze, the passengers became increasingly restive, irritating each other by the useless repetition of guesses as to when the wind might pick up.

Henrietta tried to enjoy the view around them—the ship was anchored in sight of the orange-yellow sandstone cliffs of North Head, and the deep blue of the harbour was glittering with sunshine—but its beauty was as stale as a long-stared at painting. She found herself mulling over her last conversation with Griffith. She was sure, wasn't she, that the costs and risks of her journey were worthwhile? She could have stayed, and she and Griffith would have gone on as they had done over the last two years since the death of Sir Giles Wood.

The little house Edmund had leased for her was big enough for her needs. The part-pension, as delayed as it was in being granted, was barely enough to keep the servants and—if she economised—a carriage.

She stopped still, glaring at the empty rigging before resuming her stride, going over her arguments once again. The tiny pension was transparently insufficient for a woman of her position. And so much time had gone by between the time of Sir Giles's death and the time they granted it, and they hadn't even made allowance for that period in the amount she was allocated. The long delay and the mounting debts had only added to her grief. The government coffers could afford it—after all, before he'd died, when they still thought he might manage the journey to England to restore his health, the Legislative Council had voted £2000 for his expenses. Where was that money? Did they think those expenses vanished on the day he died? And why did the widows of the Chief Justices get allocated a pension so much less than the widows of the past governors? She and Lady Ferris had supported their husbands through years of health-crushing labour at the service of the people of New South Wales. No explanation had been provided to either of them as to why they were only allowed the part-pension.

A cry went up from the sailors.

A breeze on her face and then a sudden gust pushed at her bonnet. She held the ribbon tight, closing her eyes to enjoy the rush of air on her face. No, she was right to go to London, she must put her case to the Secretary of State for War and the Colonies, and if that took leverage, well, so be it. And then, she'd be able to send Griffith the money to pay his debts, and perhaps he could come and join her in London. What fun they'd have; it would be like Calcutta all over again.

Chapter 3

The sort of man I'd want in the regiment

Morgan

The smell had gradually worsened with every day they had been at sea. Morgan Mayhew didn't mind the dim light below decks, and he counted himself fortunate to not have to share a cabin, as cramped as it was. But it seemed that the cargo of hides belonging to Messrs Sapsford and Watkins, merchants of Parramatta, had been stowed in the hold directly beneath his cabin.

In the first few days of seasickness, he had barely noticed the stink, too ill to care. In the false dawn of recovery, he had dismissed it as nothing of concern—though he had spent most of the day on deck and had drunk sufficient grog to sleep undisturbed. With the series of gales, he had succumbed once more and, confined to his cabin, the stench of the hides permeated everything—pillow, bed linen and blankets. His clothes had begun to smell as though he had been out mustering cattle. The smell of live cattle was rich and when mixed with the smells of the bush and sweat, it was the right kind of smell.

The smell in the cabin, however, was close and stale and suffocating.

He forced himself to dress. Shaving he would forego—in weather that was this unpleasant, the ladies were unlikely to be on deck.

Gordon was standing out of the brunt of the wind. He tapped his pipe on the heel of his shoe to clear it.

'Is no one else about?' asked Morgan.

'If you mean the ladies, there's been nae sight of them.' Gordon began the ritual of packing the pipe from his leather pouch of tobacco, shielding the bowl from the wind and wet. 'Dempster was about earlier, but he found the sea spray on his clothes to be a wee bit vexing.' Gordon snorted. 'Not the sort of man I'd want in the regiment.'

Morgan wondered if he would measure up to Gordon's standards of a fellow worthy of the 99th. On his way to the colony eight years before, he wouldn't have warranted so much as a glance from a hard-worn Scotsman such as Lieutenant Gordon. Back then, the cosseting of his aunts showed in his white skin, his soft hands and his fastidious manners. In contrast, the lieutenant's skin was weathered by his time with the regiment in Moreton Bay, and he was every bit the soldier. He had got himself a leg wound in the Hutt Valley campaign in New Zealand and carried himself with an air of battle-hardened weariness.

The high seas prevented much conversation—they kept a hold of the rail as the ship rose and plummeted through the waves.

'What sort of weather did you have on your passage out?' Gordon shouted above the roar.

'Mixed,' Morgan shouted back.

In fact, the voyage out in the *Mary Anne* had been marked by fine weather, but that hadn't stopped his seasickness. His shared cabin deep in the bowels of the ship had allowed no glimpse out to the water. Everyone had assured him that the remedy was to get out on deck. Then, he'd been too locked in misery to take their advice.

This voyage, he'd promised himself, would be different. He was no callow youth, even though the way Lady Wood talked to him insinuated it.

The sailors ran to and fro, drenched and shouting. Catching sight of the cook, Morgan realised that all hands were on deck and the thrill turned to fear.

'This is something, isn't it,' growled Gordon, his pipe clenched between his teeth unlit.

Morgan nodded, his eyes squinting to keep the spray out. Left to himself, he would have gone below. He might even have considered praying. He glanced again at Gordon—whooping as a particularly large wave mounted before them.

Morgan clutched at the slippery rail. A man didn't go below unless ordered. Surely seven years in the colony meant that he could call himself a man, whatever Lady Wood might think.

The transition from boy to man went unremarked for most, but Morgan knew the exact day it happened—race day at Captain Scott's estate of Bengalla …

The sheds were surrounded by carts, wagons and carriages from the surrounding district. There were lots of Scotts, along with the Ogilvies of Merton, some Bells with attractive daughters, the Bettingtons, McDougalls, Glennies, as well as the Burbridges of course. Many of the property owners lived in Sydney, and their sons were left to make a go of it, or not—as the case may be. A race day was a chance for horsetrading of all sorts, and all the hands on the properties were there too.

Morgan had felt the first bite of the summer sun in the late spring air. He remembered how he had nervously adjusted his broad-brimmed bush hat. It had still been in the same shape as the day he had bought it, unlike the weathered and battered hats that passed him. He had come up from Sydney with the Mannings, at the urging of his brother-in-law, Godfrey Wright. Morgan would have felt more at ease in the company of his cousins, David and Frank Ferris, but they were already working the property on the Darling Downs. His own journey to work the property with them had been due to start the following week—so he'd been newly outfitted and kitted up for the bush.

As they'd walked nearer to the track, the dust rose as about six horses galloped past, the sound of their hooves a pounding undercurrent to the sharp cracks of the whips and shouting of the riders. The picnicking ladies had held handkerchiefs to their noses and laughingly wiped their eyes.

'They've got a race for everything,' Godfrey had said, staring at the sketchy printed leaflet that served as the day's program. 'One for two-year-olds, one for all ages, a Hack race, and there's even a race for gentlemen riders.'

'So you'll be riding then, Mayhew.'

The deep voice had come from a short distance. When the dust cleared, Morgan had seen that the question, if it had indeed been a question, had been put by Edmund Wood, who worked a property nearby. Edmund was about his own age, long faced and outwardly sombre—Aunt Clara had introduced Morgan to the Wood family shortly after his arrival in the colony, but it had taken Morgan a while to recognise Edmund's quiet, dry humour.

Not entirely sure if he was serious, Morgan had replied, 'If there's a mount free, I'll have a shot.'

'Burbridge's brought a few over from Fordwich.' Edmund had headed off to where the dust was thickest.

Morgan had just been able to make out the melee of horses of different colours and sizes being walked about, groomed, petted and cursed by the men leading them.

'Good man,' Godfrey had said, slapping him on the back.

'What about you, then?' Morgan had said, trying to sound brave.

'I'll be too busy placing my bets.'

'For or against me?'

They had walked slowly, picking their way through the crowd towards where Edmund was standing beside an ugly stockhorse, the reins held by Bill Burbridge. A cloud had scudded across the sun, and Morgan had shivered.

He had only met Bill once before, despite the frequent parties he had attended with his aunt, where the pretty Burbridge sisters had brightened the room. Bill was built solidly like his father, for whom he was named, but lacked the penetrating stare, for which Morgan was grateful.

'Peter should do you,' Bill had said, sizing Morgan up. 'You've ridden before, I hope?'

Morgan had not had the chance to ride since he had been in the colony. Aunt Clara went everywhere by carriage, and he had decided to delay buying a horse until he was up in Queensland. But the opportunity to ride had been one of the drawcards of the colony. Morgan had tried to bolster his courage by recalling his childhood in Jamaica and being lifted into the saddle by Cudjoe, his black face splitting into a grin as Morgan nearly tipped over the other side.

'It's been a while though.'

'Well, take it easy then. There are no prizes for falling. He'll go the mile without the need of a whip. There are three heats, so pace him—I don't want him blown.'

Edmund had handed over the lead to Morgan. 'They'll be up in a minute. Go and see Dan, he'll sort you out,' he'd said, jerking his head behind him. 'Better get your bets placed, Wise.'

Morgan had walked the horse over to where they were assembling for weighing. A bluff, portly man had introduced himself as the local doctor and his mount as Melancholy. Frank Allmann, the red-faced police magistrate of Muswellbrook, had sat perched on top Flambeau, a skittish colt who had been side-stepping as if in a parade.

Morgan had stepped up to be weighed.

'You'll be flying off that horse if we don't weigh you down,' Dan, a rough stockman, had said. 'You got to be eleven stone to race.' He'd thrust two double-shot belts at him, 'Here, round your waist.'

Morgan's arm had dropped under the unexpected weight.

As Dan had helped strap the belts on him, Allman had pranced past, Flambeau's head reined back hard.

Dan had grunted. 'He's desperate to win this year—Bundock, over there on Planet; he's the favourite. But Ogilvie, there on the chestnut Pickle, he won on him last year.'

'Who will you have money on?' Morgan had asked.

'Ah well, betting's a game for fools, as they say. But if I were a betting man, I'd be staying well away from young Cox on Silver Tail over there. I don't know, Stuart Russell might give Bundock a run for his money—he's riding Hair Trigger, and he's a mean horse who doesn't like to be passed.'

Feeling the weights pressing into his back, Morgan mounted. 'No bets on last place, then?' he'd asked, the quaver in his voice betraying him.

The stockman had given another grunt, his loquacity spent, and had gone over to mark the start. The line had been indeterminate but roughly aligned with a pole.

The riders had struggled for position.

Frank Allman jostled his way past. 'You've not a ghost of a chance, laddie. You might as well stay back and play with the others and let me take the lead and win,' said the police magistrate, manoeuvring to the inside.

Morgan had found himself at the outside. He had leant forward to pat Peter's neck.

At the gunshot, they'd started. Morgan had glimpsed Godfrey waving a small slip of paper at him frantically.

'Steady Peter, old boy,' Morgan had murmured to the horse as the rest of the field moved ahead.

He'd kept him back—keeping the distance at a couple of yards as they made the first turn, marked by an old, wooden dray. The horses had been tightly packed, but he had been able to see that Allman had drawn neck and neck with Russell on Hair Trigger. Peter had been straining forward, and as they had approached the wattle tree marking the second turn, Morgan had let him have his head. In what had seemed like no time at all they had overtaken the scrum and closed in on the two leaders.

Morgan had been out of breath, but Peter's neck had stretched out, starting to enjoy himself. Russell had fallen back, and Morgan had heard over the thudding of the hooves the shouts coming from the throng gathered by the finish line. Then he had got past Russell.

Flambeau had still been ahead, lathered with sweat. Flecks of blood flew back from where each flick of the whip cut. Allman had glanced back over his shoulder, his face a purpled sheen, before flicking the whip again. It had caught Peter. Peter had lunged forward, and within seconds there had been no one in the race beside them and only Dan standing with his pole at the finish.

It's only a heat, he'd told himself. But as Godfrey had bounded over congratulating him, and Edmund had volunteered to walk Peter around for him to cool him down, and even Burbridge had smiled a little, he'd begun to enjoy the moment.

Allman had glowered as he'd wiped his face with his neckerchief. He'd stalked off to down an ale before the second heat.

Stuart Russell had come up to congratulate Morgan. 'If it can't be me, then I'm glad it's not Allman. But watch yourself in the next heat; we know you're coming up behind us now.'

Godfrey had abandoned him to reorganise his betting.

In the second heat, he'd let Peter take charge—clearly the horse knew what he was about. It had been a comfortable ride, and at the finish he'd been several yards ahead of the rest. Flambeau had trailed the field, Allman's curses and lashes making no difference. The third heat had been the toughest—it had got down to only Ogilvie on Pickle, Russell on Hair Trigger and himself on Peter. He'd been the betting favourite by then, and amid the shouting and hollering from the crowd, he'd heard Godfrey screaming with excitement.

Past the wattle tree and in front by five lengths, he'd reached for his whip and held it between his teeth as he passed the finishing post.

Burbridge had clapped him on the shoulder and said he'd be welcome to come over to Fordwich any time, and he'd heard Wood extolling the finer points of Morgan's horsemanship to the Misses Bell.

'Not bad for a new chum,' Godfrey had said, stowing his roll of bank notes.

'Who? You or me?' Morgan had replied.

Morgan smiled at the memory. *A lawyer's clerk no more. A man among men.*

On the heaving deck, Gordon swore as he tried yet again to light his pipe. 'Damn the thing.'

Morgan thought he caught the sound of Gordon's teeth chattering. His own skin was icy, and he feared that his grip on the rail might fail. He didn't trust his voice not to shake, so he simply nodded vigorously in sympathy.

'To hell with Mrs Sapsford, if I want a pipe in the cuddy, then damn me, I will.' Gordon thrust his pipe into the recesses of his greatcoat and turned to seek shelter.

Morgan held out another five minutes before joining him in the fuggy warmth of the cuddy. If Gordon could refuse to be swayed by Mrs Sapsford's sensibilities, then he could refuse Lady Wood's.

Chapter 4

A suitable ally

Henrietta

With a gasp, she woke abruptly.

Outside, the gale continued unabated as the ship heaved its way through the ocean. In the gloom, she saw water flooding under the cabin door. The ship lurched and the water receded, only to return with the next heaving roll. She sat up, fighting to push the dream aside. Her hand pressed against her mouth to hold back another wave of nausea. She wouldn't think of it. She wedged herself in the corner of the bunk, her eyes fixed on the chink of dawn light showing through the shuttered porthole, resigned to wait out the storm.

By morning, only an inch of water remained in her cabin. The dream gnawed at her and she shivered, despite her shawls and blankets. Henrietta shook her head, annoyed. She couldn't see why she was dwelling on such black thoughts. Marooned on the bunk, Henrietta watched as Hill stooped to scoop up the wet clothes and blankets from the floor into her arms. Hill kept up a stream of complaints as she worked.

'The captain, he won't like having all this drying out on deck, milady. That James, he got a right telling off when he put out all the McPhails' bedding first thing this morning. The captain said this weren't no immigrant ship.'

Henrietta snapped, 'If it's good enough for the McPhails, it's good enough for us, Hill. If you have any trouble with Captain Gallagher, tell him to take it up with me.' She swung her legs over the side of the bunk but hesitated to put her bare feet to the boards. 'And get the steward to mop up the rest of this water.'

Later, after James had swabbed out the cabin, Hill set to putting Henrietta's hair to rights. Henrietta preferred the modern fashion of letting her natural curls cluster around her face. However, refusing to move with the times, Hill pulled and tugged her hair into submission, leaving a few stray wisps to curl about her ears. Henrietta decided it wasn't worth the fight, given her hair disappeared into her widow's bonnet. Besides, it wasn't as if anyone would take a second glance at a forty-seven-year-old woman. With a vigorous movement, Hill's brush threatened to pull her eyebrows upward into a permanent look of surprise. Henrietta suppressed a groan.

'Did you not sleep well, milady?'

'Not well at all.'

'Not the same dream, the one about all the cholera and them dead bodies floating in the river in India? Like I said, milady, it's a portent.'

'Nonsense, Hill. It's the seasickness. I'm nearly over the worst.'

Hill made clucking noise with her tongue by way of repeating her statement.

Henrietta ignored her. 'Think what you like, but I don't want to dream of it anymore. And if something dreadful is going to happen, let it be quick. At least then I could get a decent night's rest.'

Hill's efforts resulted in enough dry clothing to make Henrietta presentable for her first appearance in company since they'd set sail. Although the wind was cold, the sky was a clear shimmering blue and had tempted several of her fellow passengers to enjoy the chance to take the air.

Henrietta paused as she adjusted her dark-grey bonnet, gauging her conversational options. As much as she loved being on the sea, one disadvantage was being confined in cramped spaces with the type of company that might be tolerable for an evening but which could become profoundly irritating for four months. She almost missed the privacy of the veil that she had been so glad to cast aside as she entered the final stages of mourning.

Above her, high on the poop deck, several gentlemen leant on the rail looking out to sea, the wind flapping at their coats. Old Mr Quigley was making his way up and down behind them, seemingly lost in thought.

On the quarterdeck, Mrs Berkeley was attempting to marshal her seven young children into some semblance of good behaviour with the help of her servant girl. Thankfully there was no sign of Mrs Sapsford, who generally tended to stay close by Mrs Berkeley, perhaps hoping that respectability could rub off.

Mrs Berkeley caught her up on the ship's gossip while they watched the children playing a game of quoits. Victoria, the eight-year-old, reminded Henrietta of her own Elizabeth at the same age—all energy and confidence one moment and, the next moment, cuddling into her mother for comfort. The twin boys at six were tearaways—forever finding new things to try and often suffering the consequences, just like her sons Arthur and Alec.

In a moment of sudden silence, she realised Mrs Berkeley was waiting for her to respond. 'So sorry, Mrs Berkeley, I was momentarily distracted.'

Mrs Berkeley repeated her information, speaking in a low voice so the children might not hear. 'Poor Mrs Sapsford, did no one tell you about it? Her little one died a few days out.'

Henrietta felt the chill of the whipping wind pass down her spine. 'No, I was too indisposed to be disturbed. Hill has been with me day and night, of course. The youngest wouldn't have been three, would she?'

'The seasickness was too much for her. She was very ill and, in the end, she died of exhaustion, Mr

Akers said, even though I'm sure Mrs Sapsford gave her every care.'

'Yes, yes, I'm sure Mr Akers did all he could.' Henrietta tried not to let her doubts surface about Mrs Sapsford's maternal care. 'And the funeral?' she asked.

'Captain Gallagher read the service. Mr Quigley said a prayer before they let the poor little mite down into the sea.'

Mrs Berkeley dabbed at a small tear while Henrietta looked away. She was imagining what Hill would say when she found out—that tongue of hers would likely cluck loud enough to lay an egg.

Mrs Berkeley went on. 'It all would have gone off quite well, but the captain and the first mate, Mr Jackson, started a row about which day it was that she passed, for the log you know. Afterwards, Mr Berkeley had a few words to say about it, I can tell you—'

But Henrietta didn't get to hear Mr Berkeley's opinions on the conduct of the captain and the mate, as Mrs McPhail and her daughter were upon them.

'Lady Wood, how are you feeling? Over the worst?' asked Mrs McPhail. Her brow furrowed as she continued speaking without waiting for an answer. 'Hasn't the weather been a trial? Our cabins were deluged with water in the gale. We were up all night, and the bedding was saturated. Bridget and I ended up in dear Mrs Sapsford's cabin—so kind of her under the circumstances.'

'But Mama, don't you remember, the steward told us that the water came into Lady Wood's cabin too?'

Mrs McPhail hissed to her daughter. 'I dare say a flooded cabin is managed easily when you travel with your own servant.'

Miss McPhail had the grace to look embarrassed.

Henrietta turned to see that some of the gentlemen were making their way down, although Mr Quigley continued his slow walk to and fro. Mr Mayhew, patting his remaining hair back across his scalp after the wind up on the poop deck, fell behind Lieutenant Gordon and Mr Dempster. As the three of them accommodated the ocean swell, they walked with a comradely swagger reminiscent of The Three Musketeers. She reminded herself to have as little to do with Lieutenant Gordon as she could manage.

'So you survived the flood, Lady Wood?' Mr Dempster's light hazel eyes traced her figure, despite the muted greys of her dress.

Henrietta felt he didn't mind that she noticed the direction of his gaze.

'Lady Wood is an experienced traveller, Dempster,' said Lieutenant Gordon. 'She'll not be minding a wee bit of damp.'

'It's not a matter to be dismissed, Lieutenant,' said Mrs McPhail. 'Water everywhere is very injurious to the health—Mr McPhail, God rest his soul, always used to say that there was cholera in water.'

'With all due respect, Mrs McPhail,' Lieutenant Gordon said, 'everyone knows you get cholera from breathing contaminated air.'

'When I was in India,' said Henrietta, 'and the disease first struck Calcutta, all the natives blamed the Europeans. They said we'd poisoned the water to rid the town of anyone who wasn't a Christian and to make it easier for the bishop to convert those who were left. There was a native witch who was brought up before the magistrate for predicting the deaths of all the Europeans in Calcutta. Mr Eliott, the magistrate, died of the cholera himself, not a week later.'

'So, did he get it from the water or the curse?' said Mr Mayhew.

'Well, perhaps it was the curse on the Church,' said Henrietta, pushing aside her annoyance at his impertinence. 'Calcutta's bishops did keep on dying. First there was Bishop Middleton, so tall and handsome too. They said that he died of sunstroke, but everyone knew that human hair had been cut up finely and put in his food. It coated his stomach and he died. Next was Bishop Heber, and he lasted just three years—they found him dead in his bath, with nothing to explain it. But—'

'But any number of reasons.' Mr Mayhew raised a quizzical eyebrow.

'Well, even after I left Calcutta, the bishops continued to die,' Henrietta said, determined to finish her tale, in spite of him. 'Why, a year later, there was

Bishop James. He was only forty-two. When he fell ill, the doctors told him to take a voyage. He still died and was buried at sea, poor man. And Bishop Turner came next. He was dead within a couple of years. And even—'

'Well, I hope our cabin dries out,' interrupted Mrs McPhail. 'Mr Dempster, might I impose and take advantage of your arm to have a walk about. I don't have my sea legs yet.' She tucked her hand in the crook of the elbow he offered with a hint of a bow. 'Bridget, take Mr Dempster's other arm, you don't want to fall.'

Bridget, who had been chatting with Lieutenant Gordon, gave a start and then followed her mother's instruction.

There was a momentary lull in the conversation as Lieutenant Gordon watched the McPhails moving aft with Mr Dempster, and then he applied himself to packing his pipe.

In the pause, Henrietta searched for something to break the tension. 'So, Mr Mayhew, have you enjoyed further success as a horseman since last we met?'

'What's this, Mayhew? Hiding your light under a bushel?' Lieutenant Gordon asked. 'Though, now you mention it Lady Wood, he has something of the jockey in the lightness of his build, though his height is against him.'

Mr Mayhew, his neck reddening, replied, 'Not at all.'

'My stepson, Mr Edmund Wood, was there on the race day, and he says it was the most exciting race they had seen for many years,' said Henrietta, embarrassed by her fit of pique. With Mr Dempster's attention fixated on the not-so-young Bridget McPhail, she might not be able to charm him into helping her. So that left Mr Morgan Mayhew as her only potential ally.

'All right,' said Mr Mayhew, thawing. 'You did ask, Gordon, you know. There was a picnic race day at Captain Scott's estate out at Bengalla ...' he began.

He told the story well, but Henrietta had heard it before. She sized him up as he talked. He was a light build and about her height but, she thought, he carried himself well and had a certain air about him that made him seem taller than he was. It was only in situations such as this, as he stood beside Lieutenant Gordon, that his stature was noticeable.

'Oh, well done,' she exclaimed automatically at intervals.

Mr Mayhew smiled in appreciation. 'So by the final, the crowd was cheering us on and I crossed the finishing line well ahead of the pack, holding my whip in my mouth.'

'Well, the few who had a bet on you were cheering, anyway,' said Lieutenant Gordon.

His good humour evaporated as the McPhails and Mr Dempster turned and headed back in their direction.

'The race may not be to the swift, Gordon,' Mr Mayhew said in an undertone. 'Perhaps the trick is to talk less with the filly and more with the mare.'

'I'm thinking you'll not be so experienced with horseracing that I should be listening to advice from you, laddie.' Lieutenant Gordon growled into the bowl of his pipe as he set about lighting it, his hands cupped as a shield from the wind.

'What's all this about horseracing?' asked Mr Dempster.

Miss McPhail made a discrete movement to pull away from his side, but Mr Dempster had her hand imprisoned on one arm by dint of clamping it down with his other hand. Mrs McPhail, swaying a little, managed to stand beside them, unsupported.

'I was just saying that Mr Quigley is a veritable Jorrocks, the way he races up and down the poop,' said Lieutenant Gordon.

Their eyes followed his and there were general chuckles.

Henrietta couldn't imagine a description more in contrast to the elderly gentleman's steady shuffle and stooped back.

'Jorrocks may be everyone else's favourite racehorse,' said Mr Dempster with an air of gloom. 'But not mine.'

'What? Don't tell me you bet against him?' said Mr Mayhew. 'Thirty wins from thirty-one starts last year alone.'

Lieutenant Gordon hooted. 'You had something on him at the Maitland races, then?' He slapped Mr Dempster hard on the back. 'Never mind, you weren't the only person to bet on the one he lost, after all.'

The conversation remain fixed on horseracing, a topic Henrietta could stay interested in for only so long. The McPhails also stayed, although Henrietta got the impression that Miss McPhail had been anchored to the listening post by her mother.

As Mr Dempster and Lieutenant Gordon continued to debate the relative merits of different horses, Henrietta turned to Mr Mayhew. 'Arthur has often told me what a storyteller you are, Mr Mayhew, and I see that he's right,' she said.

'You are kind to say so, Lady Wood. It's always a pleasure to remember that day, though I'm sure Arthur has heard the tale several times more than he would wish.' He paused before adding quietly, 'You know, I think that was the first day that I felt that I could make a home in New South Wales.'

Intrigued, Henrietta hoped he would go on.

However, Mrs Berkeley interrupted and said, 'Have you checked on your budgerigars today, Mr Mayhew? We've lost two.'

'It's the damp, Mrs Berkeley,' interjected Mrs McPhail. 'The poor things' feet are continually wet. No wonder they all up and die.'

'The *Lord Henderson* may be as fast a ship as Captain Gallagher says, but it's certainly a damp one,' said Mr Mayhew. 'My budgerigars—'

'I couldn't agree more,' said Mrs McPhail. 'After that gale, our cabin was flooded—completely awash. All our things sodden and—'

As Mrs McPhail warmed to her subject, Mrs Berkeley remained the only one still maintaining the appearance of listening.

Mr Dempster raised an eyebrow and said in Mr Mayhew's ear, 'So inconveniently damp taking a cabin above deck; far better to be "between decks", as we are, where it's so much dryer.'

Henrietta cleared her throat. 'Mrs McPhail, how have you been finding the meals? I have not been well enough to eat more than a little myself. Today, however, my appetite seems much improved.'

'Well, don't get your hopes up too high, Lady Wood,' Mrs McPhail said. 'The stewards are very niggardly. The fruit pies are half empty. Yesterday I helped Joseph and Bridget first and there was no more left in the dish.'

'I fully concur, Mrs McPhail. There are never enough German sausages,' said Mr Dempster.

'You are fond of sausages, Mr Dempster, I think?' said Miss McPhail.

'Yes, indeed I am, Miss McPhail. That is perceptive of you.'

Miss McPhail dropped her gaze to her feet.

Was Bridget trying to flirt? As transparent as her flirtation had been, it had apparently been effective, if Mr Dempster's flattery were anything to go on.

'It is hard to miss noticing your fondness for them, Dempster,' Mr Mayhew said, 'given that it is rare for a sausage not to have lost its ends before they reach the rest of us at the table.'

Mrs Berkeley was continuing her own line of thought. 'And the tea, really it is of the worst description.'

'All this talk about food has made me hungry,' said Mrs McPhail. 'The children should be finished their meal soon. Bridget, it is time we dressed for dinner.'

As they followed the others leaving the deck, Mr Mayhew murmured to Henrietta, 'I don't know if you like sausages, but—'

Henrietta looked at him, puzzled.

He continued, 'Young Spencer tells me that the chief steward has developed a scheme to discover who is cutting off the ends of the sausages. He has plans to put an emetic in the ends to find the culprit out.'

Henrietta smiled. She was beginning to warm to Mr Mayhew. He might at least provide some amusement for the voyage, even though he was too impossibly gauche to consider approaching about her mission, should the need arise. But if neither Mr Dempster nor Mr Mayhew, then who? If it hadn't been for Griffith's warning, she would have considered Lieutenant Gordon. His manners might be rough, but he was a man who'd weathered a few storms and navigated his way through any number of scrapes.

If only Griffith had been able to tell her more about why he was suspicious of Lieutenant Gordon, she could assess the risk herself. But, assuming that Griffith was right, the talents that would have made Lieutenant Gordon a suitable ally were the ones that made him a man to beware.

Chapter 5

One of the pall bearers

Henrietta

For the gentlemen, the dress adopted for dinner on board was the usual colonial compromise of black tails and starched collar while leaving their trousers unmatched. Now they were underway, the clean-shaven had begun to let their daily shaving ritual lapse, and so the male company was starting to gain a certain disreputable appearance. The ladies continued to make an effort but, in the absence of any younger women—since on any reasonable estimate, the number of years that Miss McPhail had been out in society must have been almost as many as she had spent in childhood—the colour range and styles were disappointing.

Most of the passengers were over their seasickness and making up for lost eating time. They were joined by Captain Gallagher and the surgeon, Mr Akers. Mr Veitch gave his excuses for his wife, who continued to be indisposed, and he proceeded to monopolise the attention of the unmarried gentlemen: Mr Dempster, Mr Mayhew and Lieutenant Gordon.

Henrietta found Mr Berkeley as uninspired a conversationalist as ever and was sorry when Mrs Berkeley took her leave to check on the children.

Mr and Mrs Owens were largely ignored, except as needed to pass dishes along. Mrs Owens sat with her hands clasped, her late stage of pregnancy poorly disguised by her voluminous skirts. From time to time, she arched her back and shifted her position in discomfort. Early in the evening, Mr Owens helped her below to her cabin and didn't return.

During dinner, Henrietta tracked Mr Dempster's movements near the sausages; however, it appeared he had thought better of his errant ways in light of Mr Mayhew's earlier teasing.

By the time the stewards cleared the table, the conversation had become argumentative.

Captain Gallagher's voice rose as he said, 'If we in New South Wales continue to refuse to take any more convicts, where else will they go? England will go back to the days of the hulks, and where will that leave the shipping companies?' He reached for more claret.

'I don't think you need worry about your job, Captain,' said Lieutenant Gordon. 'Didn't the *Lord Henderson* bring another boatload of convicts recently? Oh, excuse me, they call them "exiles" these days.'

'Yes, but the problem is why convicts are transported in the first place,' Mr Akers said.

'To my mind, there's nae punishment left in being sent to New South Wales,' Lieutenant Gordon continued. 'It's an easy life in the sunshine for them. All these exiles have to do is promise not to go back, and they get a pardon. Let them become a soldier and see what hardship is.'

Mr Berkeley cleared his throat and spoke ponderously, 'The colony's issues are not the same as those of the mother country. With the increasing cost of land imposed through the Colonial Office …'

Henrietta's mind wandered. She had heard it all before. Such debates were like food and drink to her father, William Burbridge. Stubborn, convinced of his entitlements and status as a Kentish gentleman, he was vehemently opposed to the settlement remaining a penal colony.

Mr Berkeley droned on, 'And once the new settlers realise they get more work in one day out of a free labourer than in a week with a convict, they'll soon change their minds …'

Like her father, Mr Berkeley's formulations were so slow that his listeners had long anticipated his conclusions before he reached them. Henrietta's hands fidgeted in her lap.

The captain looked set to resume his argument, but Mr Quigley spoke before him.

'Transportation has been, at least for some, an opportunity for redemption.' The tones of the lay preacher rose and fell with the slow roll of the ship.

'And, with the new Pentonville system, the pardoned exiles are reported to becoming model citizens.'

'Discipline, that's the key to Pentonville's success,' said Mr Veitch, 'and there should be more of it.'

Lieutenant Gordon spoke over the top of him. 'The Pentonvillians, you mean,' he said, emphasising the last part of the word, to general guffaws. 'A convict's a convict, no matter what the government decides to call them.'

Mr Quigley went on in his slow singsong way, undeterred. 'There are many emancipists who have made better lives and enjoy the same rights as other men. Think of Dr Bland, a member of your own profession, Mr Akers, who is a well-respected citizen. I recall reading in the *Herald* that he was one of the pall bearers at Sir Giles Wood's funeral, was he not?'

Henrietta was so taken aback at the reference to her late second husband that for a moment she was lost for words.

With a sympathetic glance in her direction, Mr Mayhew interjected, 'Dr Bland was always a gentleman, even though convicted. And surely, gentlemen, we should not bore the ladies with politics.'

'I concur,' said Mr Dempster. 'I'm sure Miss McPhail, at least, would far prefer a game of whist.'

Mrs McPhail replied on her daughter's behalf, 'Yes, indeed. Who else would like to play?'

The captain left them to their entertainment, and both Mr Quigley and Mr Veitch retired for the night. Mr Mayhew joined the game of whist, and Mr Sapsford was clearly working hard to lose his game of chess with Mr Berkeley.

Henrietta tried not to listen to Lieutenant Gordon as he regaled young Joseph McPhail with stories of his exploits at Moreton Bay, keeping his voice loud enough for Miss McPhail to hear.

Henrietta struggled to settle to her copy of the *Pickwick Papers*, one of her favourites. She'd turned over three pages and hadn't taken in a word. Mr Quigley's ill-judged remark had lodged in her mind. She found herself dwelling on the details of Sir Giles' death nearly two years before.

Over the years, she had always been the one to minister to the family when they were unwell. She prided herself on her care for her children through the fevers of Calcutta, and she glowed with satisfaction when those on the Aylesford estate nicknamed her 'Doctor'. However, faced with the loss of Sir Giles, she was paralysed. She had not known what to do, and when the nurse asked her a question or sought the smallest aid, she had been uncertain, afraid—terrified that by her own action she might hasten the end.

Dr Bland had come and gone during those long days and longer nights—always patting her hand but offering no hope. Of course, there had been no hope.

Dear Giles was worn out by the constant work in the Supreme Court.

If there were a point of law, it must be Chief Justice Wood who was consulted.

If there were a case that might cause problems with the Colonial Office, who else would take it — Chief Justice Wood, working evening after evening until late.

And if Chief Justice Wood were dying under the yoke of office, why then—his requests for leave were nothing to Governor Gipps, who refused him until it was clear to all that Chief Justice Wood couldn't go on.

Their passage on the ship home was booked, the cabin was fitted out for the comfort of Sir Giles, but it was all too late. He lay on the bed, barely able to speak, his breathing laboured. For a few days, it appeared he might recover. He sat up and they had managed to get him out in the garden in the fresh air. But the asthmatic affection worsened and his body shook, trying to grasp each breath one by one.

Edmund came down from the property at Dungog to be by his father's side. Long-faced and stern, he stood by Henrietta's chair through the long vigil. Sir Giles' daughters were both unable to travel due to their confinements. The letters from his younger son, James Sheen Wood, were brought to her the moment the ship bearing the London mail arrived. She had read them aloud to him, but she didn't know that he had heard, although he became quieter.

The long, slow procession of over a hundred carriages and thousands of mourners wound up the hill to St James' Church and onward to the burial ground on the clifftop. The sea-spray blew up from the base of the cliffs. The damp had clung to her clothes. For days afterwards, she would catch the sharp, salty smell.

It was the same smell that surrounded her now.

She couldn't help wondering what he would think of her current predicament. A philosophical man, with Whiggish leanings, he'd probably tell her to be content with her lot. He had never cared for maintaining appearances and had allocated more attention to the Supreme Court than to their financial situation.

After their debts had been paid, there was little left for his widow. Of course, he'd abhor her embarking on her present mission. Although it was being carried out with the full knowledge of Governor Gipps, such a clandestine path would have brought his censure. But, she thought, cracking the spine of her book to flatten the page open before her, as he had made no provision for her, what else could she do but take matters into her own hands?

She drew a deep breath and resumed her reading.

Alone in her cabin, she took her time preparing for bed. The hour grew late and she became more apprehensive about falling asleep and the prospect of having the same dream about cholera again. The years she lived in

India seemed another lifetime ago. She buried herself under the bedding.

From below came a loud inarticulate scream. Startled, she fought her way through the heavy blankets to a sitting position. Another cry cut through the sound of the waves, louder this time. This time she recognised the despairing tone for what it was—Mrs Owens was labouring to give birth. She lay back down and, in the lulls between cries, tried to read as the hours struggled to pass.

At least Mrs Owens is experienced, having had three children. There came another great series of bellows. *And, at least Mrs Owens has a reliable servant.*

The ship held its breath, and then came the thin, mewling cries of the newborn. Henrietta smiled. It was futile to worry about what lay ahead. Perhaps it didn't matter that Morgan Mayhew was no match for a man like Lieutenant Gordon. He too might well have strengths he had not tested.

As she settled back into the pillows, the thought struck her that Mrs Owens might have been the unintended recipient of the wrong end of the sausages. No doubt, that would have expedited matters.

Chapter 6

Iceberg ahoy!

Morgan

Lady Wood was later than usual in making her appearance on deck and, to his irritation, Morgan couldn't stop continually looking to see if she had emerged.

The voyage home was proving to be infinitely more enjoyable than his trip out. Back then, the ship had been packed with Irish Roman Catholic emigrants, and it was with some discomfort he had found out that his cabin mate, Dan O'Sullivan, was Roman Catholic too. At the end of a cramped, noisy and long journey, he had been glad to leave Dan's incipient whiskers and scrawny neck behind him.

In contrast, the *Lord Henderson* had just over a dozen cabin passengers, with the rest of the ship given over to cargo bound for England. Instead of stepping his way past the rowdy groups of emigrants, it was most enjoyable to be able to move about serenely on deck, rugged up against the icy winds as they sailed towards the southern-most tip of South America, stopping to talk every so often with the other passengers.

There were far too many children, of course. The Berkeley's youngest four played well enough with the three young Sapsfords, mimicking the pecking order of their parents, which sorted out most of their disputes. As usual, Mrs Veitch was nowhere to be seen, and so the young Veitch boy and the two Owens' children spent their days fighting and running about, always underfoot.

Mrs Berkeley's servant had the knack of keeping the girls in check. The Owens' servant, a rough capable woman, was the only one with some hope of managing the boys. Unfortunately, she was much occupied assisting with the latest addition to the family, and so the boys were running riot. Old Mr Quigley left the deck, muttering darkly about the need for more discipline, to seek the relative quiet of his cabin.

Morgan glanced again at the entrance way. Still no sign: *is she unwell?*

If asked, he would have been hard pressed to explain quite why he was so keen to see her. As each day of the voyage went by, he knew that inevitably he would find himself bested in any conversation with Lady Wood. He had lost count of the number of times she had reduced him to blush as if he were still a youth. Despite this, she was still quite the most interesting person on the ship. He fancied she had passed what his aunt would describe, in hushed tones, as *her grand climacteric*, but her face and figure were as pleasing as ever.

On the quarterdeck, Captain Gallagher had drawn a small group of passengers around him to hear him talk about the sorts of sea-life to be found this far south. After delivering a slow and tedious lecture, he was answering their questions with his usual lack of graciousness.

'Will we see any southern right whales, Captain Gallagher?' young Joseph McPhail asked.

Mrs McPhail's plump face glowed with pride as her son produced the whale's correct name, and she turned expectantly for the captain's answer.

Mr Veitch was there before him. 'We might well catch a glimpse. As I was saying to Mrs Veitch this morning, they'll be heading up north to breed—there's a large breeding ground at the Valdes Peninsula.'

As he mentioned breeding, Mr Veitch cast a disapproving look to the deck below where Mr Dempster and Miss McPhail were sitting close by each other.

Frowning, the captain spoke, ignoring Mr Veitch's interruption, 'On our way over from England we saw a lot of them in the Bight, but you'll need to keep a sharp lookout to see them on this trip.'

Morgan noticed with some surprise that Mrs Sapsford was among the passengers listening to the captain's talk. She was looking remarkably well for a mother whose young child had been buried at sea not a month since. Despite the cold weather, she had left her shawl loose, exposing her décolletage to the elements. Mr Sapsford stood behind her, oblivious. Morgan pulled his eyes away and saw the second mate, Mr Nash, who was behind the wheel beckoning the captain.

'Sir? Captain Gallagher, sir?' thirteen-year-old Charley Berkeley asked hesitantly. 'Will we see icebergs, sir?'

The captain, catching sight of Nash's efforts to attract his attention, said brusquely, 'Time to be finishing up. Work to be done.'

'But will we, Captain?' This time it was the Berkeley's eleven-year-old, Adelaide. She had a worried expression on her face.

'Yes, indeed we will,' said Mrs Sapsford, disregarding the captain. 'Before we left, Bishop Broughton assured us that we could see icebergs at this time of year. Didn't he, Mr Sapsford?'

Mr Sapsford groped for a response. He had been gazing out to sea, no doubt bored by the captain's talk. 'Indeed, Mrs Sapsford,' he said with his braying laugh.

The captain's rough face hardened and he headed off to attend to the second mate's increasingly insistent hand signals. Mr Sapsford took his opportunity to flee the lecture. He moved away from the little group to join Mr Berkeley and Mr Owens, who were deep in conversation on the forecastle.

Morgan caught a movement out of the corner of his eye and turned, but it was only Gordon, looking rather the worse for wear. The evening before had not gone well for him. He had lost at loo, as his judgement had faded with each glass of claret. Gordon, usually of an unruffled temper, proved to be a nasty drunk and, as a result, the game had ended sooner than Morgan would have liked.

'If I might have a word?' asked Gordon. 'Perhaps somewhere a bit less public.'

Curious, Morgan followed him down to the main deck and they stood, leaning against the side of a deckhouse. Morgan closed his eyes and enjoyed the warmth of the sun in the shelter out of the fresh wind.

'So, what do you think Dempster's up to?' Gordon blurted.

Morgan opened his eyes in surprise. 'Up to?'

'He's been stuck like a barnacle to Miss McPhail the whole trip. I can't imagine she's really the lass for him,' Gordon said. 'Wealthy, I mean.'

'Perhaps he likes her,' said Morgan, unconvincingly. 'We're all getting on in life—a man's got to settle down sometime, and she seems a sensible sort of girl.'

Gordon snorted.

Morgan was not sure whether he was disputing Miss McPhail's disposition or her stage of life.

Gordon tried again. 'Old McPhail must have left them well off though—cabin passengers and all.'

Uncomfortable, Morgan shrugged and laughed. 'Well, let's see if we can prise them apart.'

When they reached the couple, Mr Dempster was seated facing Miss McPhail, sketching her likeness. Morgan sat down nearby. He was struck as always by the confidence with which Mr Dempster approached every activity—a confidence that often bore no relation to his competence in its performance.

'You've missed your calling, Dempster. I shall be lining up to be your next subject,' said Gordon.

'With what end in mind?' Mr Dempster answered, not looking away from his sketching, 'Just in case the New South Wales constabulary needs a picture next time they are seeking your whereabouts?'

Gordon took the jibe in good part, possibly even flattered. He was barely managing to open his eyes beyond slits as he shielded them from the glare of the day with his hand. 'It's a bright blue sky, and on a day like today, the best place to be would be up on the forecastle, but I'll be damned if I can endure any more of that toady Sapsford.'

Miss McPhail gave a kind of hiccough as she obviously sought to suppress a giggle, covering her mouth with her hand.

'No, no that won't do at all, Miss McPhail,' Mr Dempster reprimanded. 'I can't draw what I can't see, can I?'

The ship was tacking, and a sudden blast of cold wind engulfed them.

'Quite the wake-up tonic,' Gordon said, while hugging his coat more tightly. 'No doubt Lady Wood has more sense than the rest of us and has decided to remain in the warm snug of her cabin.'

At the mention of her name, Morgan checked the entrance again.

'Settle down, Mayhew. You're like a puppy waiting for its mistress.' Mr Dempster's voice was a little too loud. 'Don't laugh, Miss McPhail, I'll lose your expression.'

Miss McPhail dutifully pressed her lips together, but as soon as Mr Dempster's eyes had fallen to his drawing, she said, 'She'll be taking time with her dress—she's out of mourning today.' At the blank incomprehension of the men, she continued, 'Chief Justice Wood passed on two and a half years ago in September. I remember because there was such a long piece about it in the paper, though I didn't attend, of course. So it is April, isn't it, so she's out of mourning.' Miss McPhail's tone suggested this to be entirely obvious.

'For the life of me, I've never understood how one can be in mourning one day and out the next,' said Mr Dempster, looking into Miss McPhail's eyes. 'One's emotions are not a tap, which can be turned on and off by the calendar.'

Gordon coughed into his hand.

Mr Dempster went on. 'I'm sure if I had the good fortune to marry and then was unfortunate enough to lose my wife, I would mourn her loss forever.' Mr Dempster sounded like he might continue in the same vein, but Miss McPhail was following the direction of Morgan's gaze.

Lady Wood had emerged into the sunshine.

'Oh, she does look lovely, doesn't she,' Miss McPhail said with a sigh.

Morgan rose to his feet. He didn't know what it was exactly that was different in her attire, since Lady Wood was as decorous as ever. Perhaps it was the thick, warm material that reflected its glow onto her complexion, or the rich depth in the colouring of the winter bonnet that framed her face, but it was a pleasure to see her.

Lady Wood stepped gracefully over to greet them and smiled at Mr Dempster's sketch. 'A most faithful likeness indeed, Mr Dempster. Nearly as alike to its owner as the one Miss McPhail did of you, yesterday. Have Miss McPhail's talents as an artist inspired you?'

In truth, the flattering portrait was more in the order of an out-and-out lie, since it bore so little resemblance to Miss McPhail's actual face. However, Mr Dempster's skill with a pen was surprisingly proficient. The similarity far exceeded the awkwardly executed likeness, which Miss McPhail had drawn of Mr Dempster the previous day.

Miss McPhail blushed with pleasure, but Mr Dempster complained of the interruptions that were preventing the picture's completion.

As Gordon led Lady Wood and Morgan away from the artist and his subject, Lady Wood took Morgan's arm. 'Does your Miss Butler draw, Mr Mayhew?'

'As a girl she enjoyed painting a great deal. She asked me to bring back some Australian birds for her to paint for our aunt as a goodbye gift, when we leave. Though at this rate, I'll be lucky if any of the budgerigars survive—two more dead this morning.' He paused to collect himself. 'Though of course I have not seen any of her work since I left England, but Aunt Mary Ann says she is very accomplished.'

'My sisters are wonderful artists but, despite my mother's best efforts, my own attempts are pitiful,' said Lady Wood.

'Perhaps Miss Burbridge and Miss Beth are so skilful because they have had more leisure to spend on their interests, unlike yourself as a married woman.'

'I'm sure you mean to be gallant, Mr Mayhew, but I assure you it is my poor skill that has diminished my application, rather than the other way around.'

Morgan brushed his moustache lightly with his forefinger. 'I, I meant, with the duties of the household and the demands of children—' He broke off uncertain how to continue, looking to Gordon for assistance.

Gordon seemed amused at his discomfort and remained silent.

Lady Wood pursued her point. 'If Miss Butler has talent, then I'm sure you will encourage her to pursue her painting after you are married, will you not?' There was a glint of challenge in her eye.

He was spared an answer by the loud yell of the captain.

'Iceberg ahoy!' Captain Gallagher shouted from the stern of the ship down to the passengers, his arm outstretched, pointing ahead.

Those nearest the captain rushed to the rails of the quarterdeck, craning their necks in every direction. Mr Veitch grabbed the collars of Adelaide Berkeley and her brother Charley as they threatened to lean right over the water. Mrs Sapsford's shawl flapped, in danger of flying off, much to the delight of Joseph McPhail, who was standing beside her. Gordon, Morgan and Lady Wood quickened their pace, moving forward towards the forecastle, where Mr Berkeley, Mr Sapsford and Mr Owens were looking about them uncertain as to the cause of the panic.

The captain yelled again, 'Iceberg ahoy!'

Mrs Berkeley and her servant struggled to prevent the younger children climbing up to the forecastle. Mr Dempster and Miss McPhail abandoned their artwork and caught up with Gordon and Morgan.

Morgan felt Lady Wood's hand slip from the crook of his arm. She raced ahead, easily outstripping him. Morgan fought the impulse to race after her. There was more joy in watching her, as light as a deer, making her way up to the forecastle. She stopped by the raid beside Berkeley, Sapsford and Veitch, her head moving from side to side as she scanned the horizon.

Breathless, Morgan and the others joined them.

'Can you see it, Mr Mayhew? Mr Berkeley thought for a moment that he had, but it was only a low cloud.' Lady Wood pointed out to sea.

'Where does the captain say it is?' Morgan asked, starting to turn his head towards the stern.

The small distant figure of the captain was doubled over. It took a few seconds, but then they realised he was laughing as he slapped Mr Nash heartily on the back.

Gordon groaned. 'It's the first of April, of course.'

Mr Dempster and Miss McPhail paused, still halfway up the steps to the forecastle. Mr Dempster moved up a step to stand close to steady her.

They saw the realisation spread through the passengers grouped on the quarterdeck, and Mrs McPhail called down to Mrs Berkeley not to be concerned. 'Just the captain's little joke, nothing to be alarmed about.'

Mr Berkeley's complexion had turned purple, and Mr Sapsford tutted. 'Fool of a man. Upsetting the women and children like that.'

On the other hand, in different company, Mr Owens might have laughed out loud. However, in deference to his betters, he gripped the rail while his shoulders shook silently. Morgan waited anxiously for Lady Wood's reaction.

'Such a disappointment,' she said. 'I thought we were going to have an adventure.'

He was trying to formulate some similarly light response when she turned away from him to approach Mr Nash.

Annoyed at his slowness, he hovered at the top of the steps as the others left the forecastle. Gordon was already halfway back down to where Mr Dempster and Miss McPhail had descended. As Morgan commenced his descent, he glanced back to see that Lady Wood had taken possession of Mr Nash's telescope and was scanning the horizon. Perhaps she hoped to spy a real iceberg, though she was directing her attention back the way they'd come, following Mr Nash's directions.

Mr Sapsford held out his arm to assist Mrs Sapsford while she came down from the quarterdeck. As usual, she lifted her gaudy skirts higher than necessary as she stepped down. Gordon was enjoying the view from below and gave Morgan a sly wink. But, as lovely as her fine ankles were, her waspish nature took away any pleasure in her company as far as he was concerned.

Mrs Sapsford appeared to have taken the captain's joke very personally. 'Lady Wood should not give any attention to such foolishness,' she complained, not bothering to lower her voice. 'Laughing like that, it can only encourage the captain even further. It was not amusing of him to mock us all, making us rush about like so many chickens.'

Mr Sapsford murmured his agreement.

Mrs Sapsford said, 'Though why I should expect any dignity from that direction, I don't know, given the eccentricities of her late husband.'

Even Mr Sapsford recognised his wife was overstepping the bounds. He twisted his neck around in an attempt to check if they had been overheard. 'There, there Mrs Sapsford, the late Chief Justice Wood might have been Irish in company, but he was always a proper Englishman on the Bench.' He took his wife's elbow and, in a discrete effort to silence her, deftly steered her closer to join Mr Hall and the Berkeleys, who were trying to explain the April Fool to the children.

However, once the steam train of Mrs Sapsford's vituperation had begun, it was difficult to stop, with interruption only serving to result in her switching tracks.

'That's as may be, Mr Sapsford, but I'm sure an upright young man like Mr Mayhew here would agree that there were a lot of questions left unanswered at the time of his death.' She tossed her head.

Morgan glanced in the direction of where Lady Wood was making her way down from the forecastle, horrified she might catch the drift of conversation on the wind. Mr Sapsford seemed to be at a loss as to how to put an end to her comments.

Morgan opened his mouth to speak but didn't manage to utter a sound before Mrs Sapsford continued, 'Well, if the Chief Justice of the Supreme Court isn't responsible for the proper conduct of the officers of the court, then who is? First it was old Mr Manning, the Registrar of the Court of all people, making free with the Intestate Estates fund. Then, only a couple of years later, it was Macquoid as Sheriff of the Court being charged with fraud. At least young Mr Macquoid did the right thing, undertaking to pay his father's creditors back even after his father took his own life.'

'I do not know that Macquoid is so worthy of the praise which you and the general public seem to think important to bestow upon him,' Morgan interrupted. 'The arrangement with his father's creditors means he can keep his livelihood by working on the property, so at least some degree of self-interest is involved.' Morgan felt the inadequacy of his comment. Mrs Sapsford had attacked so many targets, it was hard to know which to defend. Besides, he might distract her from comments about Chief Justice Wood and Lady Wood.

He expected Mr Sapsford to assist his efforts to derail his wife's indiscreet remarks, but Mr Sapsford had taken the opportunity of Morgan's interruption to quietly move aside. He was taking an unusual degree of interest in a conversation between Miss McPhail and Mr Dempster, who were standing by the rail.

Gordon cleared his throat, preparing to air his thoughts.

Mrs Sapsford was too quick for him. 'Bishop Broughton was discussing the matter with Mr Sapsford and myself only shortly before we left. What's your authority for your comments Mr Mayhew?'

Shocked by her abrupt and nasty tone, Morgan decided not to mention that he had heard the stories of both old Manning's and Macquoid's defalcations through his friend Godfrey Wright. The last thing he wanted was to provide Mrs Sapsford with further objects for her invective. Instead, he simply said, 'Myself.'

'Well, as I said, I beg to differ with your opinion,' she retorted.

Morgan had had enough. 'Macquoid is by way of being a neighbour, as his property is in the Tuggeranong and mine in Yass.' He addressed his comments to Mr Berkeley, who had wandered over, perhaps with a view of quelling the dispute. 'I do not mean to imply any improper behaviour on his part, but through the arrangement with the creditors, he is able to support himself and his aunt. This being the case, I feel it is reasonable to impute that his motivation for the arrangement arises from the wish to achieve that goal rather than from any particular self-denying impulse to compensate for his father's deficiencies.'

Mrs Sapsford's complexion coloured, perhaps only now realising their conversation had an audience, including Mr Berkeley. She stammered, 'Oh, I was talking about the situation before, when he lived by himself, of course.'

As they made their way from the deck, Morgan felt a gentle pat on his arm.

'That was very brave of you,' Henrietta murmured.

'I'm sorry you overheard,' he said. 'I had been hoping you were out of earshot.'

'She was certainly in fine voice, wasn't she? I always find that since no one ever pays her any credence, it is generally best to leave her to confirm her lack of acumen to her listeners.'

Chapter 7

Sweethearts and wives

Morgan

Morgan continued to nurse his irritation about his argument with Mrs Sapsford. Despite venting his feelings in his diary, which usually proved calming, by early afternoon, he decided he couldn't let matters go. He went on deck, determined to have a word with Mr Sapsford about his wife's rudeness.

Most of the passengers were taking the air, but as they were grouped together, he saw that he'd have to hold his tongue for the present.

'So, Mr Berkeley, are we still to read the play after our dinner?' asked Mrs Berkeley.

Morgan's ears pricked up. The play had provided much conversation over much of the previous week. The usual activities of whist and loo after dinner were proving expensive for some passengers, and so their frequency had waned. However, without activity, the gentlemen were drinking heavily, and the ladies were complaining.

Old Mr Quigley, Mr Veitch and Mr Berkeley were frequent volunteers to read aloud. Since their choices were guided by their preparation for the readings they undertook for the service on alternate Sundays, their offers were declined more often than not.

Mr Owens thought well of his singing voice, and he and Mrs McPhail could be relied upon for a song. In Morgan's opinion at least, the finer features of most duets were lost as they tried to out-do each other in loudness.

To general acclaim, Mrs McPhail had suggested they might read a play.

There had ensued much debate as to which play might suit, until it was realised that in fact there were only two copies of plays on board. Mr Akers, the ship's doctor, was reading *Faust,* but it turned out to be in German. Young Joseph McPhail confessed to a copy of *Sweethearts and Wives,* though he blushed to own it.

There was general enthusiasm for the light romantic farce, since many of them knew the songs. Some of them, including the Sapsfords and the Owens, had seen it performed at the Royal Victoria Theatre only a few years before. Of course, there were mutterings about propriety from Mr Quigley and Mr Veitch, although Mr Berkeley had condescended to consider the matter.

'Mr Berkeley?' his wife repeated, her smile tense.

'As long as the children are in bed, then I am happy for it to proceed,' he announced.

'Oh, but the older ones could stay up for the occasion?' Mrs Berkeley said. 'Charley and Adelaide were so looking forward to hearing it.' She took a deep breath. 'Perhaps if you and I were to read the parts of Eugenia and Charles, it would be perfectly proper? After all, they are meant to be really married in the play, aren't they, even if no one knows it at first?'

Gordon guffawed. 'Thank you, Mrs Berkeley. I shall be able to excuse myself from listening, now I know the end.'

'Oh, I've spoiled it.' She looked distraught.

'Not at all, dear Mrs Berkeley,' Mrs McPhail said. 'That fact comes out early on in the play. And I think if you are taking the part of Eugenia, my Bridget would make a wonderful Laura, don't you agree?'

Mr Dempster was standing beside the blushing Miss McPhail. 'Yes, wonderful,' he said. 'And I can be Sandford to Miss McPhail's Laura.'

'No, no, I couldn't,' Miss McPhail cried.

'I think I should be just right for Laura,' said Mrs Sapsford, 'Don't you think, Mr Sapsford.' She glanced flirtatiously in Mr Dempster's direction.

Mr Dempster turned to Morgan. 'Now I come to reflect upon it, I think Mr Mayhew would be an excellent choice for Laura's Sandford.'

Morgan stared at him, catching Mrs Sapsford's furious expression out of the corner of his eye.

Mr Dempster ignored them both. 'I see myself as more of a Charles Franklin to your Eugenia, what do you think, Mrs Berkeley?'

Mr Berkeley cleared his throat. 'Mrs Berkeley may need to step out during the play to attend to the children. I think we will make a much better audience than be among the players.'

Mrs Berkeley's face fell.

Mr Sapsford turned to his wife. 'Perhaps dear ...' But he didn't get to finish.

'I shall read Eugenia and Mr Sapsford can read Charles Franklin; that would be entirely proper,' said Mrs Sapsford.

Mr Sapsford gave her the look only married couples can give—that look which promises further discussion at a later time.

Mrs McPhail was turning in confusion from one to the other as the roles rapidly switched players. She was transparently desperate for her daughter to have a part. 'And Bridget can be Susan. That's a young woman's part.' She glared around her as if daring any of the women, all of whom were older, to dispute this.

Mr Dempster immediately spoke up and said, 'Since I'm not to be Charles or Sandford, I shall be most pleased to read the part of Billy Lackaday.'

Knowing the play ended with Billy proposing to Susan meant that Miss McPhail's pink face deepened its hue.

Mrs McPhail smiled to herself as she moved on to organise the remaining parts. She allocated her son Joseph McPhail in his absence to the role of Curtis. Her eye fell on Lady Wood who was inquiring from Mr Veitch about his wife's health.

'Perhaps Lady Wood would be so gracious as to read Mrs Bell?' she called.

Lady Wood was smiling as though about to agree, while having no notion of the conversation. The thought of Lady Wood being asked to play the role of the widowed innkeeper Mrs Bell was preposterous. She would be playing opposite the young Joseph McPhail as Curtis. Morgan shook his head slightly, trying to signal her discretely.

Lady Wood paused.

'But Mrs McPhail,' said Morgan. 'You have such a fine sense of humour; you would make a delightful Mrs Bell. And I think we would have the pleasure of hearing you sing in that role, would we not?'

'But then young Joseph can't be Curtis, since Mrs Bell and Curtis are to marry by the end,' said Mrs McPhail, screwing up her face in concentration.

Gordon had been watching the negotiations with every sign of increasing vexation. With some assertion, he said, 'So, Lady Wood shall play Laura to Mr Mayhew's Sandford, and I can play your Curtis, Mrs McPhail.'

Mrs McPhail's blush almost matched that of her daughter's.

Morgan missed Lady Wood's expression, as she turned back to her conversation.

While the passengers were leaving the deck to change for dinner, he took Mr Sapsford aside. 'I'm sorry to have to mention this, Sapsford, but I think you need to have a word with Mrs Sapsford. I couldn't say more to her directly yesterday, of course, but I take offence at her contradicting me in public and suggesting, at the least, I was in error, or more probably, that I was defaming Mr Macquoid. Certainly you agree.'

Mr Sapsford frowned crossly, about to argue, but Mr Berkeley intervened as he passed. 'I'm sure Mrs Sapsford would not wish to impute any misstatement on your part, Mr Mayhew.'

Mr Sapsford's mouth twisted into an attempt at a conciliatory smile. 'She has a generous spirit, and I'm sure her only thought was that a deserving young man such as Macquoid should not be robbed of his due praise.' He moved on, clearly trying to catch up to Mr Berkeley.

Lady Wood lingered behind, engaged in talking with Mr Nash. The second mate was deep in explaining something to her in relation to the ship. When the first mate, Mr Jackson, called for his attendance on the quarterdeck to hand over the watch, Morgan waited for her to join him.

'I have now learnt more about the ship's rigging than any person other than a sailor needs to know, Mr Mayhew, and I blame you.'

His spirits lifted. 'Surely not, Lady Wood, I get the impression you are a veritable sponge for information, so I cannot see why I am at fault.'

'I was forced to stop and talk since, from my vantage point, it appeared you were rather at odds with Mr Sapsford.'

Morgan's bad mood returned. 'Mrs Sapsford's manners were the difficulty. A lady does not contradict a gentleman in public.'

'I confess I am confused. Was it being contradicted that was problematic, or that it was by a lady, or that it was in public?'

He went to reply and then, seeing the twinkle in her eyes, found himself laughing. 'None of those, but rather that it was done so ungraciously.'

'That is fortunate, Mr Mayhew, since it appears that for our play reading, I am Laura to your Sandford. If my memory of the piece serves, I shall be contradicting you mightily and in public.'

After dinner was finished in the cuddy, the stewards cleared the plates away and the younger children were packed off to be settled for the evening by the servants. The passengers set about getting ready for the reading of the play.

The area before the sideboard was declared the stage, as there was more standing room there than anywhere else. The table was too long and heavy to move aside. Instead, the stewards moved the long benches away from the table and at a slight angle so those seated could view the players.

There had been a general assumption that the captain might be prevailed upon to read the part of Admiral Franklin. Gruffly, he excused himself, citing his duties in preparation for the watch he would start at eight. Instead, old Mr Quigley agreed, so long as he could remain seated throughout. The other cast members chose to stand, despite the fall and rise of the ship.

There was only one copy of the play, so those who were to read parts grouped themselves to be close enough to hand it easily to the next reader.

In their roles as Charles Franklin and Eugenia, Mr and Mrs Sapsford stood behind Mr Quigley's chair. Miss McPhail stationed herself next to her mother, her eyes fixed on the floor in terror while stumbling over Susan's lines. Mrs McPhail entered into the spirit of the lively Mrs Bell with much gusto, frequently using her elbows to add emphasis to her speeches to Gordon in his role of Curtis. Gordon had drunk even more than usual through dinner, prompting Mr Dempster to accuse him of needing some Dutch courage. Possibly the amount he had imbibed dulled the pain of Mrs McPhail's elbows, as apart from the occasional wince, he took her emphases in good grace.

With parts for ten, their audience of only six was sparser than the players. Mrs Berkeley hung on every word, her mouth moving along with some lines, seeing as she clearly knew them well. She laughed in all the right places, every so often expending her energies by clasping the hands of her children Charley and Adelaide on either side. Mr Berkeley sat further back, occasionally permitting himself a smile.

To Morgan's surprise, he saw Mr Veitch seated beside Joseph McPhail. Perhaps Mr Quigley, being one of the players, helped him decide the frivolous entertainment was sufficiently respectable? As always, Mrs Veitch was absent, and Morgan wondered if she was avoiding their company or that of her judgemental husband.

As expected, Mr Owens joined in on all the songs exuberantly. Mrs Owens held her new baby boy swaddled tightly in her arms and jiggled him to keep him quiet. Mr Akers sat near her, stealing an indulgent peek at the tiny bundle when the players lost track of their parts, which happened often.

Mr Dempster's Billy Lackaday proved to be the audience's favourite, even prompting the occasional burst of applause, generally led by Mrs Berkeley. He wandered about the patch of stage as he enacted all his scenes. He expended most of his energies on those scenes where he was meant to be wooing Susan, much to Miss McPhail's discomfort.

Morgan decided that in his role as the sophisticated Sandford, he could lean against the sideboard to retain his balance. From time to time, he felt the pressure of Lady Wood's hand resting on his arm as she flirted with him in her role as Laura.

'I beg your pardon, I fear I disturb your solitude,' she read.

'You are too apt, madam, to disturb my solitude, and yet well know I prize your society but too highly,' Morgan replied, reading over her shoulder. He was starting to feel the part of Sandford was perhaps rather too close to the truth.

'Better than it deserves, you mean, and yet so little that I vow of late you seem determined to avoid me.' Lady Wood dropped her eyes coquettishly as she deftly passed on the copy of the play to him.

'In shunning you, madam, I deserve your acknowledgements—your cousin has arrived—Charles Franklin, the son of your uncle, and as you say, of your benefactor—I have no business here; and you ought rather to commend my discretion.' Morgan was a skilled reader, but even he found himself having to work hard.

Lady Wood laughed in an astonishingly natural manner. Apparently having already read ahead, she replied from memory. 'I admire it above all things, I protest, a more discreet young man I never met with.'

Is she asking me a question? Could he be trusted to be discrete? *But about what?* Morgan shook the thoughts out of his head and tried to sound sad as he read his next line. 'It comes a little out of season—but my error is not irreparable—tomorrow I set sail.'

'Set sail?' Her voice was tremulous, and she spoke again from memory.

Morgan found himself replying genuinely, 'You can't be surprised, madam?'

'Indeed, but I am very much surprised.'

'Impossible! There are dangers 'tis wisest to avoid.' Morgan did his best to imbue his tone with something of the gravitas of Mr Berkeley. 'Your wedding is approaching, madam—some of the family would probably be kind enough to send me an invitation, which would be equally painful to me, either to accept, or refuse.'

'But if I were to ask you to my wedding?'

Are those tears welling in her eyes? He quickly looked down to find his place. 'I should think you more unfeeling than I do at present.' Seeing her next lines were lengthy, he handed her the copy of the play.

She took it and walked a couple of paces forward in front of him to face the audience. 'You are very polite, sir, and exceedingly charitable. But go, sir, by all means—travel the wide world over, amuse yourself, and forget the friends you leave at home.'

From the way the audience laughed appreciatively at her ironic exaggeration, Morgan wondered what expression she had enacted before she continued, 'Find better, if you can, and when you've taught them to value and regret you, leave them as you do us, without a pang at parting.'

For Morgan, the rest of the play passed in a blur.

Finally, even old Quigley managed to read without sounding like a sermon as he said the Admiral's lines to Gordon as Curtis. 'And you, sir, shall serve out a jorum of grog to every blue-jacket in the harbour, to drink the seaman's good old toast, "Sweethearts and wives".'

The little audience got to their feet clapping. They picked up their glasses and drank the toast. The players rushed to the sideboard for their drinks, repeating in a ragged chorus, 'To sweethearts and wives.'

Amid the bumping rush and laughter, Lady Wood called to Mrs McPhail, 'So then, pray where does that leave us poor widows?'

Gordon reached across behind Morgan to refill his glass. He muttered in his ear, 'I do not think that that widow would say "nae" to anyone who would offer himself as a sweetheart.'

Horrified, Morgan checked to see if Lady Wood might have heard, but she had moved across to Mrs Berkeley. They were laughing at some of the questions that Charley and Adelaide were asking about the plot they seemed to have missed.

There were many congratulations all round and praise for all who had read their lines well. However, eventually the Owens retired for the evening and, at a nod from Mr Berkeley, Mrs Berkeley left with Charley and Adelaide with her. Old Mr Quigley and Mr Veitch settled into their nightly game of chess. Mr Dempster and Gordon resumed their rivalry at cards. They managed to recruit Miss McPhail and Mrs McPhail to join them for a game of whist, ignoring their protestations as it grew late.

Lady Wood's eyes were bright with the excitement of the play, and Morgan felt the same way. Despite trying to keep Gordon's earlier comment on widows out of his mind, Morgan couldn't help asking, 'When you were in India, *sati* was still being practised, was it not, Lady Wood?'

'Yes, indeed. I actually witnessed the last *sati* in Calcutta,' Lady Wood said tersely, the light in her eyes extinguished.

'The last *sati* in India, Lady Wood? Can you recall the year?' asked Mr Berkeley in the uncomfortable silence.

'It was before my children were born,' Lady Wood said. 'So perhaps 1817, I should think.'

Abruptly, Mr Sapsford chimed in, 'Well then, that couldn't have been the last time it occurred. I understood Governor-General Bentinck to be the one who outlawed the infernal practice. He was there after your time in India, wasn't he, Lady Wood?'

Morgan felt his cheeks redden at the ill manners of the man. He felt for Lady Wood, as her facts were disputed so roughly and her age highlighted at the same time.

Lady Wood's face showed barely a ripple. 'I'm sure you are both correct; however, I do recall that in 1817, the East India Company regulated against the practice of *sati*. No doubt, events that occurred later may well have disrupted the promulgation of those regulations, as you say. It was a very sacred rite to those who practised it, and so regulation was much disputed.'

Her response seemed to satisfy Mr Berkeley and Mr Sapsford, who fell to discussing the various religions with much interest, if only to themselves. Gordon called for attention to the game, and Mr Dempster and the McPhails turned back to concentrate on the cards, with young Joseph being recruited to assist by keeping track of the wins and losses.

Mr Akers drew his chair closer to Lady Wood and Morgan. 'Forgive me if I go back on a sensitive topic, Lady Wood, but when you described *sati* as a sacred rite, you weren't defending it?

Morgan had also been puzzled by her comment, but not brave enough to raise a query. He waited for her response with great interest.

'I suppose it is because of being widowed—on two occasions—that I have considered the matter. Perhaps it is some kind of fellow feeling.'

Morgan was about to acknowledge the depth of emotion by trying to steer the conversation into calmer waters, but she went on.

'You see, after the government changed the law in Bengal to give property rights to widows, the practice of *sati* was said to have increased. And even if the widow decided to live and claim the property, her failure to perform *sati* meant she was excluded from her family and friends. However, if the practice were to be honoured, then her fellow wives would at least live in honour and comfort. So these are circumstances we need to consider, don't you think, before we judge the widow's actions?'

Mr Akers nodded, clearly considering her points. 'So you're saying their choice is the devil or the deep sea.'

'Or rather, heaven or the deep sea, in their view,' Lady Wood added.

'Thank goodness our society doesn't require such things of its widows,' said Morgan.

'You think it doesn't Mr Mayhew?'

And again, Morgan felt there was another question she was asking that lay submerged beneath, but he couldn't fathom it.

Chapter 8

A widow's living death

Henrietta

Back in her cabin, Henrietta's spirits fell. So often she had told her stories of other places, other adventures, but she was tired of hearing her own voice.

She feared sleep and the dreams it would bring. The way she was feeling, she would have nightmares of being dragged to a burning pyre, screaming for somebody to fetch Lord Grey from the Colonial Office to save her.

She retrieved her book from her trunk. She'd read *Pickwick Papers* so many times she could almost recite entire passages, but Dickens never failed to soothe her. Her candle flickered, and she blinked to keep her focus on the page …

She was walking past the *dhobi wallahs*, who were bent over doing their washing by the shore near the *ghat*. She gathered her skirts out of the muddy dirt. It would be a waste of her remaining rupees to have them washed.

Not that it mattered, she wouldn't call on anyone and no one would call upon her. Calcutta society was always in constant flux, with people heading home and new hopefuls arriving. She recalled they used to say that within any seven-year period, there was a complete turnover of Europeans. With the collapsing financial markets, five years or less would be sufficient. No one she had called 'friend' was in India anymore, and no one who was still there was prepared to receive her.

She tripped and almost fell, and a brown hand reached out to her. She jerked away.

'Mrs Richeley, is that you? I did not expect to meet you here,' came the lilting accent.

She looked into the lined face of the portly gentleman swathed in white cloth, his head wrapped in a purple turban. Relief flooded her as she recognised the old *babu* who had worked with their agency for many years. 'Mr Dutt, it is indeed a pleasure to see a familiar face. I find myself in unexpected circumstances.' She found she couldn't go on—she wouldn't let herself be seen to cry in the street.

'Ah, yes. It is a sad business. But where is your husband?' he said, looking about. 'Is Mr Richeley not with you? I heard the *Katherine Stewart* was impounded. They didn't imprison Mr Richeley, surely?'

'No, no, we got word while we were still on board outside Sand Heads. The pilot ship brought the news, so Mr Richeley took the opportunity to avoid apprehension.' She paused, choosing her words. 'He's seeking to make his way back to England.'

'Very good, no doubt he will find some assistance from Mr Piggott and your aunt.' Mr Dutt must have caught a glimpse of her thoughts, as he added, 'I am sure your current difficulties will soon seem a passing dream.'

They continued to walk as they talked, navigating the jostling of the crowds as they reached the busy streets. Henrietta held her perfumed handkerchief to her nose and blinked to keep the dust out of her eyes.

'Your accommodation is nearby?' said Mr Dutt. 'It is not a good idea for a lady to be unescorted.'

Henrietta couldn't meet his eyes. 'No, no. Please, do not trouble yourself. It is a little way yet, and I would not want to take you out of your way.' She thought of the mean boarding house, and the heat prickled against her collar.

'Well then, you will do me great honour if you would allow me to provide you with a conveyance.' He gestured to some men idling by their palanquin. Before Henrietta had time to find some excuse, he had paid them for their services to take her on her way.

Arriving back at her lodgings, she was irritated to find that her maidservant was still out. Sarah Mott had taken it upon herself to explore the locality to find the best prices to stretch their meagre funds further. Sarah's disappointment, when her expectations of a world of riches in exotic Calcutta were not met, had been as bitter as Henrietta's own.

When she did get back from her shopping, she fussed over Henrietta's dress, trying to brush off the grey dirt. Henrietta sat on the bed in their cramped room, her mind vacant.

Sarah chatted away as she sponged off the worst of the mud splatters. 'And she asked for you, but you weren't here, so she said she would call again.'

Inattentive, Henrietta grasped the last part. 'What? Did you say someone called?' Her hopes of help from those she had once thought friends flickered back into life.

'The lady left her card.' Sarah rummaged in her apron pockets until she found it. She handed the card to Henrietta with a frown. 'I wasn't sure where to put it, ma'am, there being no mantelpiece or nothing.'

Henrietta read the names, shaking her head. 'I don't think I'm acquainted with a Mrs Allport.'

Sarah looked glum, unable to help. 'She was—you know, respectable. But not rich like …' Her voice tailed off.

Henrietta stayed in the boarding house the rest of the day, hoping Mrs Allport, whoever she was, might call again in the afternoon. Highly unlikely, she knew. By that time of day, if she were someone who moved in society, she and her husband would be taking a drive on The Course. But she waited all the same.

By the time she had given up, her best dress was creased, perspiration soaked into the armpits, and Sarah's goodwill was extinguished as she faced trying to repair the damage before the next morning.

It was a long and sleepless night—close and hot.

In the early light of dawn, the slightest breath of air made its way in through the small high window. Henrietta dozed, only to be woken by Sarah's movements as she began the day.

Dressed once more, Henrietta sat welded in her seat to minimise further creasing under Sarah's watchful eye. A distant knock at the door and she waited, counting the seconds, until Sarah ushered in the visitor.

Disappointed, she saw the caller wasn't the mysterious lady, but rather the *babu*, Mr Dutt. Henrietta rose, discomfited.

He bobbed his turbaned head, taking his inventory of her lodgings with each nod. He then clicked his tongue and tsked before saying, 'It is as I thought. Mrs Richeley, you find yourself in straitened circumstances. It would be my honour to provide you with all the help I can. I know you come from a proud family, Mrs Richeley.' He drew out a small canvas bag. 'But before you refuse me, I wish you to recall the many kindnesses that your husband—and before him your uncle—have done for me and my family over many years. I would consider it a great privilege if you would kindly take this gift in payment of my debt.'

Henrietta eyed the canvas bag, trying to estimate the value of its contents.

Mr Dutt continued, 'No, no I insist. I ask you to humour an old man and accept this small token of his gratitude.' He put the bag down on the dresser with an air of finality. 'We can talk more at a later time and see what else might be done to provide for your passage back to your family in Sydney.' He shook his head. 'Prices have soared with the shortage of ships—but we can see, we can see. I have friends who may be able to help. In the meantime, we need to organise you more suitable accommodation, and—'

They were interrupted by the sound of another knock on the door below.

Sarah clattered down the stairs. Light footsteps followed her back up.

'Mrs Allport, ma'am,' Sarah said. She dipped in an awkward curtsy and backed out of the room.

Mrs Allport was an older woman, at least in her forties, her dress was out of fashion but well made. At the sight of the *babu*, who had risen to greet her, she took a step back.

Henrietta mentally reviewed the available proprieties for such a situation but found little to help. 'Mrs Allport, I am sorry but I find that in my recent troubles I must have let our acquaintance slip from memory?'

'The fault is mine, Mrs Richeley,' Mrs Allport said, with a worried glance at Mr Dutt. 'Mr Allport is acquainted with your husband through their Lodge, and so he wished me to call to bring you news.'

With a deep breath, Henrietta collected herself. She said with a gesture of introduction, 'Babu Russoomay Dutt has long been a trusted adviser to our firm and to my husband. He is most keen to assist in any way he can.'

Mrs Allport inclined her head and Mr Dutt bowed.

Mrs Allport didn't look convinced. After a moment's thought, she said, 'They secured your husband a berth on the *William Young* to Liverpool, and so he has departed safely.'

Henrietta's knees buckled and she barely managed to sit without falling. 'It was so kind of you to come in person and give me the news. I would offer you some refreshment but—'

'No, no, not at all.' Mrs Allport shook her head, her gloved hands touching her mouth as if to ward off any possibility of food or drink. She cast her eyes about the shabby room. 'Mr Allport and I also wanted to let you know that you would be most welcome to stay with us.'

By that evening, Henrietta and Sarah were jolting along in the palanquin across to the other side of the Hugli River to the Allport's house in Shibpur. Henrietta recognised the streets as close to the apartments where, after they had married, she and Patrick had resided with her uncle and aunt. However, it was not until she alighted that she saw that the house they were about to enter was the same one. Still exclaiming, she found that the room Mrs Allport had provided for her use was the one she had slept in when she had lived there. She did cry then, and Mrs Allport kindly withdrew.

Months passed while she waited for a berth to Sydney.

Mrs Allport had a keen ear for gossip and was happy to bring Henrietta up to date with what she had missed in her five years' absence.

'So did you hear about the Witney blankets?' Mrs Allport said, her eyes twinkling.

'No, but I gather I soon shall.'

'Well, it was the season, and the young and not so young ladies were coming off the boats with dreams of matrimony, and all the bachelors of Calcutta were vying for the honour of eluding the chaperones and, well you know.'

Henrietta smiled, remembering herself eleven years ago—fifteen, dazzled by the parties and balls and so many young men with their eager eyes.

'Well, a gentleman who shall remain nameless, at the urging of his wife had invited two of her nieces to come out. Naturally, he gave no more thought to the matter, so when many months later his *sircar* brought him a letter, his wife asked about it. He replied, "Oh, it only tells me that the Witney blanks I ordered have come." "But, sir," says the *sircar*, "There are two young ladies waiting in the palanquin downstairs, just arrived from England."' Mrs Allport was laughing as she told the story and paused to catch her breath. 'Well, it turned out the letters from the agent in London were put into the wrong covers at the time the young ladies left for India.'

Henrietta laughed dutifully.

'And,' said Mrs Allport, with the glee of finishing off her joke, 'you'd never guess what everyone is calling them now — the Witney blankets!'

'I daresay that has improved their prospects,' Henrietta said.

They were interrupted by Mr Dutt, by now a frequent visitor to the Allport's home.

'I bring news, Mrs Richeley. I have found a berth for you on the *Marquis of Landsdowne*.' Mr Dutt shuffled his feet. 'It is a smaller ship, and I am afraid I could not purchase a passage for your servant and still ensure you the comfort of a cabin.'

Henrietta thought for a moment of Sarah's situation. Still, the girl did say she was looking for adventure.

Mr Dutt was still talking. 'But I understand the stewards are very good, very upright and proper.'

She had no other choices, but she paused as if considering the proposition, before replying, 'Yes, I am sure this is the best option. I cannot thank you enough for all your assistance.'

After he had left, she sat turning over in her mind the things she would need to do to make preparations to depart.

'You must be worrying about young Sarah,' Mrs Allport said sympathetically. 'I have a thought about that. You knew the Lindsays when you were living in Agra, didn't you? They intend to return to England soon and are looking to employ a suitable servant.'

Henrietta was sure Sarah would complain all the same. Still, she would be in safe hands with the Lindsays, and no doubt she'd be better off in the long run away from India's lonely expatriate young gentlemen …

Dimly, Henrietta heard a soft step. Her book slipped out from under her hand. 'Sarah?'

'It's me, Hill, milady. Mr Dickens must've put you to sleep.'

'I wasn't asleep,' Henrietta said, opening her eyes. 'Just remembering.'

During all the time she'd been marooned in Calcutta, she'd had no idea that she was already widowed, since news of Richeley's death had taken so long to reach her. But she'd known the poverty of widowhood and the humiliation of being cared for by strangers. *There*, she could say to Mr Mayhew, *see, Mr Mayhew, that's a tale of a widow's living death for you.*

But she dismissed the idea. She wasn't about to humiliate herself by casting herself as an object of pity. No, Mr Mayhew seemed flattered by her attentions and, if she needed to call upon him, he'd assist from sheer gallantry. And, Lieutenant Gordon had not troubled her so far. In fact, her attempts to keep him at a distance were working surprisingly well, possibly because he was distracted by competing with Mr Dempster for Miss McPhail's attentions.

But still, she thought, her mood plummeting once more—there had still been no sign of a following vessel, which would deliver her the other part of the documents. Perhaps then there might be trouble. Her only certainty was that she was determined to assure that her status and her income were never threatened again.

'Well, they'll be starting Sunday service without you if you're not careful. At this rate, you'll not be able to check on your parrots beforehand,' Hill said as she busied herself clearing away and setting the cabin to rights. 'Now, tell me if you feel an itch, Lady Wood. The Owens' children have got head lice, and it doesn't take much for them to take off in a small space. You ought to hear Mrs Sapsford on the subject. We've boiled everything they've touched and rubbed their heads with mutton fat and combed the critters out, and if that doesn't work then Mrs Sapsford is threatening to shave their heads.'

With the mention of lice, Henrietta found herself idly scratching. She couldn't stay in the close cabin a minute longer.

The coachman's tale

Morgan

'Mr Berkeley read the service so well this morning,' said Mrs McPhail.

Mrs Berkeley smiled at the compliment to her husband but kept her eyes on her needlework.

Morgan had joined Lady Wood and the other ladies when they'd made their way to the cuddy earlier than usual. The wind outside was icy despite the bright blue sky. Unfortunately, the children were still finishing their meal, and with the coming and going of servants and stewards, the cuddy was crowded and noisy.

'I always enjoy the service when Mr Berkeley reads it,' said Mrs Sapsford.

Mrs McPhail looked nervously in the direction of Mr Quigley, who alternated with Mr Berkeley in doing the readings. However, he was engrossed in his game of chess with Mr Veitch.

Mrs Sapsford mouthed, 'Deaf as a post.' She had some embroidery in her lap, but the work had barely progressed through the voyage.

Both gentlemen were intent on the game and resolutely ignoring the Owens' boy who stood nearby. The five-year-old was staring at the board, breathing heavily through his mouth, undeterred even by the Owens' servant vigorously wiping his nose.

'I am so longing to reach London.' Mrs Sapsford sallied forth with another conversational topic to engage the attention of Mrs Berkeley.

Mrs Berkeley, kind as ever, obliged. 'Yes, indeed. I'm looking forward to being able to take a carriage ride through the countryside.' She closed her eyes. 'Green pastures, hedgerows … won't that be something?'

'And no bushrangers. Papa said,' piped up the Owens' boy.

Morgan wondered if he should mention highwaymen but decided not to.

'Yes, you're right,' Mrs Berkeley said to the boy indulgently. Her hand automatically reached out to pat his head, but she rapidly withdrew it. The lice plague was ever in their minds. 'Why, Lady Wood has first-hand experience of them.'

'No, not at all,' Lady Wood said with a laugh. 'My sisters were the heroines of the hour.'

'It's not like you to miss all the fun, Lady Wood,' said Mrs Sapsford. 'Where were you when the robbery was going on?'

Lady Wood ignored her. 'It is indeed a most amusing tale. Have you not heard about it already, Mr Mayhew? Wasn't it in the papers, Mrs McPhail?'

'Oh, yes. Poor Mr Burbridge.'

'Well, I wasn't there, of course. I was in the house with my dear mama who had one of her headaches,' Lady Wood said with a nod to Mrs Sapsford. 'But I have all the details from my maid, who got it directly from the coachman—'

They all laughed, and Morgan wondered, not for the first time, how it was that Lady Wood, the most demanding of servants' time and energy, could reliably tap that rich vein of gossip.

'Well, there was our dear papa quietly returning from a day at the races when, shortly after he'd turned into the Aylesford estate, four men sprang out from the bushes and, waving their guns, hauled the coachman down and bound him. Then, holding a pistol to our father's head, they demanded all the money he had on him. So what do you think our father said to that?'

'No doubt, not something that could be repeated in present company,' said old Mr Quigley, clearly drawn into the tale from his corner.

'Well, my father said he had none about him.'

'That would've earned him a cuff about the ears at the very least,' said Morgan, in admiration.

'Well, of course, since it was race day, they'd be sure that a wealthy gentleman would be carrying more than usual. So then, they said.' And here Lady Wood affected a rough man's accent. 'You'd better 'ave a care about wot you're saying, 'cos we gonna search you and, if we find so much as a sixpenny bit more on ya than wot you said, then we'll blow your brains out on the spot.'

Even Mrs Sapsford began to laugh.

'But, no, does my father alter his story?' Lady Wood continued.

'No,' her listeners cried in answer.

'No, he doesn't. He says he had a bad day at the races and had not a penny on him. So then, they tell him to strip to the skin. But then he pleads; he is an old man and in very infirm health, and to do so might kill him. And he must have been convincing, because then they fell to arguing with each other about what they should do. All this time, what they didn't know,' Lady Wood said, lowering her voice, 'was that Jack, our stable boy, had hitched himself a ride home on the back of the carriage and he'd hopped off the moment the bushrangers sprang out. He raised the alarm up at the house.'

Miss McPhail spoke up, asking, 'But then how did—?'

Lady Wood smiled. 'Luckily, for my father, we three sisters are all proficient horsewomen. With all the men of the estate yet to return from the races, my sisters rode out to the rescue, and the robbers, intimidated by such a force of gorgons, cravenly decamped post-haste.'

Tea being served meant that the conversation turned to other more mundane matters for a while.

Miss McPhail looked puzzled by the story. 'I'm still a little confused. Did Mr Burbridge, in truth, not have any money on his person? Is he a gambling man?' she asked tentatively.

'Oh, I'm sure his pockets were bulging with money,' said Lady Wood. 'It would be so like him to plead poor while all the time secreting a fortune away. I think it's actually why I liked the coachman's tale so much. It sums up my life's experience with my dear papa.'

Chapter 10

The only currency that really mattered

Henrietta

Back in her cabin, Henrietta submitted to the tugging and pulling as Hill brushed her hair.

'We'll be doing out the cabin with carbolic tomorrow, milady. It can't wait any longer. You don't want them nits in your hair,' said Hill as she gave a vigorous tug at a knot.

'Careful, you're as bad as Sarah — I'll be bald before I'm fifty.'

Henrietta glanced towards the hatbox. *Should I leave the documents where they are, or will Hill check the contents in her efforts to hunt down contamination?* She needed to relocate them, but where?

Hill's tugging eased off a little. 'Did you ever hear from your friends in England, the ones who took Sarah? Perhaps we'll manage to see her again. I mean, I mean if I was to accompany you to their house in the country.'

Clearly, Henrietta reflected, Hill had been reading another Jane Austen novel. 'I doubt if I shall do much in the way of visiting country homes. I much prefer to explore the sights of London,' she said. And besides, it was clear that her financial circumstances were not going to be such as would put her into those circles. Seeing the disappointment on Hill's face, she added, 'I don't know that Sarah ever reached England and, if she did, it wasn't with the Lindsays. I heard that on her way to meet them in Chowringhee, she ran off with a gentleman of my acquaintance.'

Hill stopped mid-stroke.

It was too tiresome to go into details. Henrietta said, 'I'll undress myself. You can run along now.'

'But,' Hill said, obviously trying to collect herself, 'I need to fix the lamp.'

'No, no leave it. The steward can fill it later.'

Hill hurried out the door, no doubt to return to her reading, thought Henrietta.

She had to retrieve the documents and find a safer hiding place. If she asked, surely Mr Mayhew would tuck them away in his cabin for a short while. She began to adjust the lamp. Immediately, it fluttered out. Maddeningly, there was no oil left.

She threw her shawl around her shoulders and made her way back to the now empty cuddy where John, the chief steward, was still clearing up.

He followed her to her cabin, but after he checked the lamp, he declared, 'The bowl is too warm to fill again, milady. I'll tell Spencer to come up and sort it out for you in a little while.'

'Leave the oil, I'll get Hill to see to it shortly,' she said, taking the lamp back from him.

After he left, she set about relighting it herself.

The flame flared high, startling her so that she knocked her hand against it. She grasped the glass before it fell. The burn shot through her fingertips. For a long second her hand fused to the lamp, before she could release her grip. She cradled her fingers with her other hand, bent almost double in agony. She rocked forward and back until the pain receded enough for her to think of a remedy.

The pitcher of water sat by her bed, and she thrust her hand into it.

When the ache subsided, she started the slow process of changing into her nightclothes one-handed, impatient with the loops and ties. Her good hand fumbled. Her fingers seemed to have lost their nimbleness.

She stretched her fingers. Unconsciously, the burned hand moved in synchrony. She plunged it back into the water to feel the salve of the numbing coolness.

Sitting still, memories stirred and rose unbidden to the surface.

The tide of despair, which swamped her that day so long ago, washed over her as she sat half-undressed, perched on the edge of the bed with her hand in the pitcher

Her mind wandered back to her last outbound voyage back to Calcutta on the *Katherine Stewart* with Patrick …

Despite the wrench of leaving the children in Sydney, she had been glad to leave. Sydney was empty without Baron Hyacinthe de Bougainville.

Patrick was drinking heavily, the long four years of their separation unable to be bridged in the confines of their cabin.

They were no sooner out of Port Jackson than he told her.

The agency was in difficulties. The company of Piggott, Davidson, Robertson and Richeley was under financial strain. He planned to wind up his affairs and get out while he could. They could go back to England, back to the colony, wherever she wanted. But they wouldn't be able to stay in Calcutta.

Finally, she understood—why the drinking, why he had spent all his time in Sydney doing deals to buy property, why he didn't want to bring the children with them. But as it transpired, he failed to recognise the extent of the financial collapse.

At Sand Heads, the pilot boat brought him a message from his fellow masons from the Star-in-the-East lodge. Their letter carried the news. With Uncle Piggott and Mr Robertson long returned to England, and Davidson preoccupied with his interests in

Canton, Patrick alone remained for the creditors to chase. The letter urged him to flee to the other side of the Mahratta Ditch, where British law didn't apply and where his passage on a ship would be arranged.

She had one last glimpse of the top of his head as he scrambled down the side of the ship to join the pilot at Sand Heads to make his escape from prosecution. Barely a goodbye.

A year and a half later, long after she made it back to Sydney, she heard news of him. Patrick had died within a fortnight of leaving India …

She shook off the thought and gingerly sucked each fingertip in turn before she continued to get ready for bed.

She tossed and turned, shivering cold one minute and sweating with a burning heat the next, plagued by distorted dreams …

She stood on deck next to the captain. The fire-worshipping steward, stripped to the waist, struggled with the ropes that tied his wrists above him to the mast. He had been taller than the man who had bound him, and his long, brown arms were strong, the sinews etched across his skin as he wrestled with the ropes. With a cry he broke free, and with one desperate look around him, for a brief moment silhouetted against the late afternoon sky, he sprang over the side.

She ran to the rail but the ship's officers were there before her. She could hear shouts and splashes. By the time there was a space for her to wriggle through, the boats had been lowered to save him.

The steward swam away, strongly at first. The sailors shouted, but the man kept swimming. A trail of blood from his back stained the water in his wake.

Then the man in the sea was Patrick—not Patrick as she had last seen him, red-faced and stout with too much wine, but young, handsome Patrick.

He lifted his arm in the air to her. His deep voice rang across the waves. 'Do you think to save me? Never! My character is ruined, what have I to live for?'

He swam on.

Each time the boats came near, he dived under the water to escape their outstretched arms. Eventually, the men ceased rowing and watched silently. He kept swimming until she could only make out the shape of his head, black against the setting sun on the horizon. At last, it sank from view …

Gasping, Henrietta threw off the blankets and sat up, cradling her burned hand aching with pain. Her memories tugged at her as she fought to free herself of their weight.

Maybe talking with Miss McPhail caused them to reawaken. She didn't want to think about her last months with Patrick. They were so inextricably wound up with those precious few days with de Bougainville. Such a gallant Frenchman, so charming. Perhaps she meant nothing to him. Perhaps her sister's betrayal had simply provided him with a convenient way to extricate himself from their affair. And, in the end, her husband had insisted: her reputation was all she had.

She couldn't have known then that her reputation was on the brink of ruin, albeit in a different sense. And a few months later, bankruptcy stripped her of the only currency that really mattered—her social standing.

The door opened and the wind blew in the rest of the gentlemen. With them came the smell of tobacco and whiskey.

'Get away from it.' Mr Owens shoved his son out of the way.

Mr Berkeley signalled to his children, and they wriggled off the benches, the other children following suit.

The servants herded them below, allowing the little ones who were still eating to bring along fistfuls of bread. The stewards cleared the table, working around the passengers who began to be seated.

'I tell you, Gordon,' said the captain, continuing an argument that had been going on for some time. 'The quality of the diamonds coming out of Brazil put those that used to come from India to shame.'

Lieutenant Gordon looked tired of the discussion and shook his head, exchanging a private smile with Miss McPhail.

'It's more in the cut,' said Mr Dempster authoritatively. 'If the stone isn't cut in Amsterdam, they are not going to hold their value.'

'That's exactly what Mr McPhail always said, isn't it Bridget?' said Mrs McPhail in enthusiastic agreement.

Miss McPhail nodded dutifully.

'I know a chap who said he'd come across diamonds in South Africa,' said Mr Owens.

There was a general guffaw. James, the assistant steward, busily sponging off the table fought back a smirk.

'Not likely,' said Mr Sapsford. 'Why that's about as ludicrous as saying we'll be finding gold in Australia.'

They all laughed, and Mrs Sapsford leaned over towards Captain Gallagher, the movement exaggerating her cleavage. 'So, have you got one of these Brazilian diamonds to show us?'

'Certainly I have,' the captain said. 'I won a tiepin off a fellow when we were in Sydney—worth at least fifteen guineas when we reach London.'

Morgan whistled under his breath in astonishment and glanced over to Lady Wood.

'Mr Berkeley, didn't you say you were bringing with you that diamond ring of your grandmothers for you niece?' asked Mrs Sapsford. 'How much would you say it was worth?'

Mr Berkeley looked embarrassed at the question. 'It has been valued at something of that order.'

Mr Dempster said, 'Well, I say we need to judge the difference for ourselves. I'm a good judge of such things. Bring them both out for inspection.'

The captain strode off to get the pin, entering the passageway at the same time as James. The assistant steward, carrying a heavy tub of warm water, was pushed off balance. The tub was caught between the two of them, wedging itself deeply back into James' side before finally tipping and falling, drenching the captain's trousers.

'What's wrong with you, boy?' shouted the captain. 'At the drink again?'

James quickly scrambled to his feet, pressing his back against the passage wall. 'No, sir. Sorry, sir.'

After the captain had passed, James bent over to retrieve the tub, wincing as he did so.

Mrs Berkeley rose. 'I'll just check on the children. Shall I fetch the ring for you, Mr Berkeley?'

'You would have seen some fine diamonds while you were in India, would you not, Lady Wood?' Morgan asked.

There was a perceptible snort from Mrs Sapsford, but Henrietta ignored her. 'Yes, indeed. But for myself, diamonds hold little attraction. There is something cold about them, don't you think? All sparkle and ice.'

'Down in Yass, when the mid-winter frosts hit, you'd swear the ground was covered in diamonds,' Morgan said.

'Very poetic of you, Mayhew,' said Lieutenant Gordon. 'I've only been through Yass once, and that was one time too many.'

'I prefer pearls—I have a lovely seed pearl necklace that I was given in Batavia,' Henrietta shared.

'But they say they're unlucky,' said Miss McPhail.

'Well, they weren't for the giver,' she replied with a hint of mischief. 'He was the richest man I ever encountered. On my return from Calcutta for the last time, the Marquis of Landsdowne had to pick up cargo in Batavia. I was introduced to Mr and Mrs Stewart, who took me to visit the home of an enormously rich Dutch gentleman—they described him as the Rothschild of the island.'

'I think I've heard of him,' said Mr Veitch said. 'The bastard son of a Dutch merchant, mother was a slave? Dutch government borrowed vast sums of money from the father during the war with England and paid him back with a grant of land that they thought was useless. Is that the chap?'

'That was the story I was told,' said Henrietta, with a twinkle in her eye at Mr Veitch's outrage. 'Apparently, he knew all along that the land included an area where the terns nest in their million and—'

Lieutenant Gordon interrupted and said, 'I hear those birds make nests bring in a pretty penny in China.'

'He made his fortune by selling their nests in Canton,' said Henrietta, her eyes glazing over as she remembered. 'On entering the hall of his mansion, sweet Italian music was being played by a band of sixty musicians in the outer veranda. While we were listening to this, there came twelve young girls dressed in the finest white Dacca muslin, their waists confined by rings of pure gold, their wrists wreathed in bracelets of jewels, and wearing splendid earrings. One girl carried a silver tray covered with scarlet velvet on which was coffee in outer cups of gold filigree, with Sevre china. The next girl followed with liqueurs in exquisite bottles and glasses, then came another girl with fruits, preserves and cakes, and on it went, each girl presenting a different offering. As we left, I saw a dozen or more carriages of every form and description in the coach houses, some in the shape of boats, and one a peacock with the tail spread, and another shaped like a nautilus shell.' She shook her head as though to clear it.

'But how did you come to be given the pearl necklace,' snapped Mrs Sapsford impatiently.

Henrietta shrugged. 'I don't think it was of any consequence for him. He offered us a bowl of what he described as trinkets—full of precious and semi-precious jewellery—we could select whatever we liked.'

Mrs Sapsford harrumphed. 'Well, diamonds would have been a better choice.'

Mrs Berkeley returned before Captain Gallagher. She handed the ring first to Mr Berkeley who passed it around for inspection. 'Poor James is not well,' she whispered to Henrietta. 'The chief steward says that he may have cracked a rib and perhaps has suffered some internal injury. But Mr Akers has been called to see to him. He might need to be bled.'

Mr Sapsford held the Berkeley's ring up to the light. 'Very fine, very fine indeed.' He handed it to Henrietta.

Captain Gallagher lumbered in, a small gold tiepin cradled in his outstretched hand to Mr Dempster. 'Here you are then, have a look at that.'

'A nice-looking piece,' said Mr Dempster, peering at the diamond at the head of the pin.

'I know a thing or two about stones, as I told you,' said the captain. 'That pin is easily worth fifteen guineas, as any valuer in London will be able to affirm.'

Mr Berkeley exchanged a look of satisfaction with Mrs Berkeley. 'We can settle the matter once we're in London, Captain, if you're prepared to back your judgement. I was planning to have the ring valued anyway.'

Mr Sapsford sniffed. 'A bit on the small size, I would have thought. I'll wager five shillings that Mr Berkeley's stone is the more valuable.'

'Ah, it's not the size, as they say,' said Lieutenant Gordon.

Repressing a smile, Mr Dempster handed the ring to Miss McPhail. 'What do you think? Would you be a happy woman to own a ring such as this?'

'I couldn't say.' Miss McPhail kept her eyes fixed on the ring. 'Which is worth more, I mean. Lady Wood might.' She passed it to Henrietta.

'Yes, given all your great experience of the riches of the East, Lady Wood,' said Mrs Sapsford, 'I'm sure you'd know better than we who have been less fortunate.'

Henrietta weighed the ring and the pin in each hand, looking from one to the other. 'They are different cuts of course, and it makes it hard to compare.' She held them up to the lamplight. 'And the light in here is very poor—it would be good to see them in the daylight. What do you think, Mr Mayhew?'

Mrs Sapsford rolled her eyes.

Mr Mayhew examined each for a long time. 'My apologies, Captain, but I'd be happy to put one pound on Mr Berkeley's being the better diamond.'

'Done,' said the captain. 'I can see that I'll be making a tidy profit from this. As soon as Mr Akers is with us, we'll have it noted in the ledger. I wouldn't want anyone forgetting. I might even be putting some of my own money on it.'

Chapter 11

The pleasure of tumbling

Henrietta

The temperature climbed as they altered course to head north. Henrietta tossed and turned in the heat of the stuffy cabin, shut up against the weather, listening to the rats. The *Lord Henderson* had moved into the main shipping lanes and there had been talk that they might begin to see some other ships. She wasn't the only passenger eager for news and the replenishment of stores. Any one of the ships they encountered might also be carrying the second packet of documents. However, if the seas remained rough, Henrietta couldn't see any likelihood of the captain sending a boat across to another ship.

She staggered with the movement of the ship as she tugged at the cabin door. Suddenly, a heavy weight fell against her. Another lurch. She was thrown back across her bunk.

'My apologies, Lady Wood.' Lieutenant Gordon, grabbing wildly about him, struggled to get to his feet. 'I was relying on the walls for stability and then your door gave way.'

Henrietta fought to push him away. She reached for the edge of the bunk. A sharp roll of the ship sent Lieutenant Gordon crashing backwards on another collision course.

'Careful as you go, milady,' Lieutenant Gordon said, hauling her upright.

Reflexively, Henrietta darted a look to her painter's box where she'd hidden the packet of documents. It had been knocked to the floor and the lid had sprung open. Bits of charcoal and grimy rags spilled out in a mess.

Lieutenant Gordon, following her gaze, dropped to his knees, his hands reaching for the rolling pots.

Henrietta, heart in her mouth, realised her mistake. 'No, no,' she said, affecting nonchalance. 'Leave it. Hill will attend to it.'

'It's no trouble. After all, it's my fault.' Lieutenant Gordon, still crouching, twisted his head towards her with a quizzical look.

'Not at all, Lieutenant.' Henrietta forced herself to smile sweetly and moved to the door. 'Are you breakfasting in the cuddy? Perhaps I could borrow your arm to steady myself?'

Lieutenant Gordon dutifully rose and held out his arm.

Coming towards them along the narrow passageway was a moving mountain of bedding, and behind it poked the head of James, the assistant steward.

'Sorry, your ladyship, we haven't been able to lay the breakfast things yet. A few of the gentlemen slept overnight in the cuddy for the cooler air, and we're not quite finished clearing them out.'

Henrietta pressed herself against the wall to let him pass. 'In that case,' she said, 'if you'll excuse me, Lieutenant Gordon, I might pop back to my cabin and get Hill to fix my hair clip. It seems to have come adrift.'

After waiting to be sure Lieutenant Gordon was headed in the direction of the cuddy, she made her way back to her cabin. She scrabbled in the painter's box until she retrieved the packet. *There has to be a better hiding place. Gordon is far too knowing.* She cast her eyes about, panicking in case Hill returned.

Her hatbox, of course! She'd only had Hill retrieve her summer hat from below the day before. She tucked the packet under the silk lining of the box and slid it back on top of her trunks.

Her mind settled, she left the cabin for Hill to restore to order. She proceeded towards the cuddy, keeping her arms stretched to either side of the passage walls for balance. The ship rolled as she entered the cuddy and, for a moment, she thought she might fall. She gasped as her hip rammed into the end of the sideboard.

Mr Mayhew was already inside, washed, dressed and looking at the empty table as if waiting for food to appear magically.

'So, Mayhew, like the rest of us, you sweated it out down below in your cabin last night,' Lieutenant Gordon was saying, as Henrietta slid into the safety of a seat, avoiding his eye.

'Not at all. I thought it was a highly practical way to escape the worst of the heat by sleeping in the cuddy, so I followed young Master McPhail's example.'

With the arrival of the stewards bearing trays of food, there was a pause in the conversation.

Mr Dempster, filling his plate with sausages, picked up the thread. 'Well, I have had a capital start to the day. I have been hearing about Gordon's morning exploits. Apparently, he had the pleasure of tumbling into Lady Wood's cabin.'

Any answer Henrietta might give would provoke embellishment. She remained silent.

'Milk, Lady Wood?' Mr Mayhew offered, coming to her rescue. 'The steward brought it up fresh from milking the ship's cow.'

'Finally. So the captain has decided that we do not have to wait until the day's cooking is done before we are permitted to drink it.' Henrietta spoke with more heat than she had intended. She knew it was not the captain's fault. As the weather had become more tropical, it was inevitable the milk soured by dinner.

The sweet taste lingering on her tongue allowed her to keep her tone even as she asked, 'So, do you know if we have passed any ships?'

'We sighted the *Berhampore* at first light,' said Mr Mayhew. 'Forty-two days out from Liverpool bound for Calcutta, and thence to Sydney. Jackson managed to get a jolly-boat across, and I was able to get a letter off for my sister. They could only let us have a barrel of flour—conserving their provisions, no doubt.'

Lieutenant Gordon groaned. 'So, still no bread for us then. What's it been, more than a week? Who went across? If it was our diplomat of a captain, no wonder that's all they were prepared to trade. Next time, I'll go across myself and strike a better deal.'

Henrietta tried to keep her face unperturbed. If Lieutenant Gordon were to collect the mail, he could intercept any package directed to her. She would have to stop him.

As the other passengers started to drift in for breakfast, the news of the *Berhampore* was passed on. The continued lack of bread was deplored by all. Even the fresh supply of milk was not enough to contain the general grumbling. Henrietta's exasperation increased with every retelling and, when Mr Dempster began his joke about Lieutenant Gordon tumbling into her cabin yet again, she left.

She had been intending to go down to check on her birds—the rainbow lorikeets were off their food and starting to worry her. However, she caught the cooling invitation of outside air and changed her mind.

The wind had shifted, blowing fresh against her face as she stood on the quarterdeck. With the change in direction, the sea was flatter. While they continued to make steady progress, she was able to walk about without losing her balance. The sailors were busy under the close eye of Captain Gallagher. Far off, she made out an approaching vessel. As the word spread, the other passengers who were eager for the novelty ahead joined her. Their excitement meant that her own agitation went unremarked.

'Yankee ship,' Lieutenant Gordon said, his eyes narrowed. 'So who's going across with me?'

'Mr Mayhew,' said Henrietta, 'you spent a considerable time in Bristol, didn't you? No doubt, you'd be very comfortable in the jolly-boat.'

'I'm sure Dempster will volunteer to do the honours,' replied Mr Mayhew.

'To impress a certain paramour, no doubt,' said Lieutenant Gordon. 'We'll see if we can make ourselves useful and get some more whiskey. Stocks are running short. We'll be down to colonial moselle next.'

'Not a bad drop.' Mr Dempster had come up behind to join them at the rail, Miss McPhail on his arm. 'I like them sweet.'

Miss McPhail giggled awkwardly.

'So you'll come across with me, Dempster?' asked Lieutenant Gordon.

Mr Dempster blanched and then recovered himself. 'In principle, of course. Love to. But not on this occasion. I've promised to spend the morning with better company.' He winked at Miss McPhail.

Henrietta stared at Mr Mayhew, willing him to volunteer.

'You're expecting mail, Lady Wood?'

She cursed inwardly. Mr Mayhew was proving to be one of the most sensitively attuned young men she'd ever met. Unfortunately, he was perhaps too alert.

She gave what she hoped was a casual shrug. 'Griffith did promise he would write, but he's always been a less than reliable correspondent. But, I confess I would like some jam, if they have any to spare.'

'Well then, jam it is,' Mr Mayhew said, with only a barely audible tremor of doubt.

'So anyone else like to place an order?' asked Lieutenant Gordon.

Mr Akers came over, bouncing on the balls of his feet, keyed up with anticipation. 'Don't take too many orders, Mr Mayhew. The steward has given us a long list. Got to leave room for the return trip to fit in the necessities and still have room for the captain. It's money up front for this little excursion.'

'No need for Mr Mayhew to go,' said Lieutenant Gordon. 'I'd be happy to break the monotony and come along.'

'Can't have the three of us taking up valuable space, now can we?' said Mr Akers. 'And you take up a lot more room than Mr Mayhew here, I have to say.'

Lieutenant Gordon looked sour and wandered away as the others gave Mr Mayhew their requests and the money they were prepared to spend. The ship proved to be the *Lenore*, bound for Calcutta.

As the *Lenore* drew closer alongside, Mrs Berkeley and her children clustered about and craned their necks for a better view. Close on the heels of Mrs Sapsford's children came the two Owens' children. Since Mr and Mrs Owens were not in sight, there was a general rush to prevent them climbing up to the rail.

'Where's young Master McPhail?' asked Henrietta, freed from her worries. 'I thought he'd be keen to watch the fun, if not go across in the boat himself.'

'He's not well, poor lad,' Mrs McPhail said. She then whispered to Henrietta, 'Some nasty boils on his ... his back,' she said. 'I've told him that Mr Akers needs to see about them, but he says he's busy.'

'No guarantees,' Mr Mayhew shouted back, reminding them, as he followed Mr Jackson and Mr Akers down the side of the ship.

Henrietta repressed a twinge of guilt at his despairing face as he clambered down the rope ladder to the jolly-boat that was tossing about on the waves far below.

Henrietta wasn't alone in pacing the deck, casting anxious glances to the *Lenore*, waiting for the return of the jolly-boat. There was general jubilation when Mr Akers staggered back on deck with the news they had obtained as much flour as needed. Henrietta followed in the wake of the other excited passengers as Mr Akers directed the mailbag to be off-loaded in the cuddy. She hovered uncertainly behind, trying not to appear too eager, all too aware of the eyes of Lieutenant Gordon.

'Lady Wood?' Mr Mayhew spoke quietly from the doorway.

Henrietta swung around excitedly, her attempts at unconcern shattered.

Mr Mayhew's complexion had a green tinge but his hand was steady as he held out a small jar of jam. 'I hope you like pineapple. It was all they were prepared to spare.'

'Oh,' she said, trying to smile. She moved toward him, turning her back to block Lieutenant Gordon's observations. 'Anything else? Any mail?'

'Nothing, I'm afraid,' Mr Mayhew said. He patted the side of his coat. 'So shall we find a spoon in the galley so you can try a little of the jam?'

Henrietta's smile came readily. 'But of course. And I think you have earned the first spoonful for your efforts.' She led the way straight to her cabin.

As soon as she closed the door, Mr Mayhew drew out another small packet and handed it to her. It was heavily wrapped to ward against moisture.

She turned it over in her hands, looking for any kind of note or even her name on it, but there was nothing. 'But how did you know it was for me?'

Mr Mayhew took a steadying breath. 'Forgive me if you think I'm presuming too much, but I got the impression that you had some particular reason for wanting me, rather than anyone else, to collect this? So, it struck me you wanted its collection to be conducted with some discretion. When we boarded, I managed to slip into our introductions that I had you to blame for my enduring the excursion. And I do lay the responsibility with you, Lady Wood, for the loss of my breakfast.' He paused a moment, smiling wanly. 'So, while Mr Akers was busying himself haggling over prices, I took a stroll about, in case anyone from the *Lenore* should be waiting for such an opportunity. Sure enough, one of the midshipmen approached and handed this over. Oh, and this.' He drew out a small, much folded note.

Henrietta grabbed it and went to open it; it was Griffith's handwriting. Abruptly she stopped. 'I can't thank you enough, Mr Mayhew, for your assistance and your … discretion.'

Mr Mayhew, thankfully, caught her meaning and left.

What he thought she was up to, she didn't know. Perhaps he thought she was receiving some kind of *billet-doux* from a secret admirer. She shook her head at her fancy. More likely he thought the debt collectors were in pursuit and she wished to hide the fact from the other passengers.

She tucked the second packet with its brother in her hatbox, vowing to find a safer place later, before sitting on her bunk to read Griffith's note.

'Sorry, sorry, milady,' said Hill, bursting through the door with James in tow.

Henrietta palmed the note in her hand so that Hill couldn't make out the writing. Hill knew Griffith's hand and would want to know all the news.

'We got to get all the bedding out in the sun. It's Mr Akers' orders, what wiv the lice and all.'

Henrietta frowned and thought of telling Hill to wait. But she'd waited this long, and Griffith probably was only admonishing her to make sure she came back soon. She'd have to be patient a little while longer.

When she returned to the cuddy, the passengers were squabbling their way through the financial complexities involved for the various delicacies they'd purchased. A mess of newspapers from London lay strewn across the table.

Mr Berkeley cleared his throat, breaking the silence. 'Sad news, I'm afraid. Governor Gipps has died.'

Henrietta's gasp was echoed by Mrs Berkeley.

Mrs Berkeley was the first to speak. 'He was so frail when he left his post, but didn't we hear that things had improved for him once he had got back to England?'

Mr Veitch and Mr Quigley spoke at once.

'Well, in my opinion, he was no loss to the colony,' Mr Veitch said.

'Worst governor we ever had,' said Mr Quigley. His voice was the louder, so he continued on at length about the Whig leanings of the former governor and his disastrous kowtowing to the Colonial Office.

Henrietta was trying to take in the implications. Gipps had promised his support for her petition to Lord Grey—this whole mission had been set up under his aegis. Would Lord Grey even know what was to be done with the documents without Gipps' briefing?

'Sad news,' said Mrs Berkeley to Henrietta, handing her the paper. 'He would have been fifty-five, I think—a man still in his prime. Poor Lady Gipps.'

Thinking about Gipps' wife was a welcome distraction. Poor Lady Gipps had pleaded ill-health throughout the eight years of her husband's office. She'd used her illness as an excuse to wriggle out of her engagements as First Lady of the colony and yet somehow had still managed to outlive her husband.

Henrietta couldn't mourn the news of his death. She stared at the newspaper, remembering the reply sent by Gipps to Sir Giles' request for leave due to ill-health: 'The colony is so soon to undergo the change from Bondage, as a penal colony to the Free Institutions of England, no other person is so duly qualified to conduct the business, and Sir Giles Wood cannot be spared'.

It didn't matter that Gipps had relented a few months later.

And now the damned governor was dead and gone and with him went her chance of her petition to shore up her financial position. So why should she even bother finding out whether she were still to pass on the documents to Lord Grey? She might as well toss the lot into the sea and be done with all the worry. She'd tell Griffith that they didn't arrive. He'd believe her.

Initially, Henrietta was alone in not sharing the elation among the passengers who were buoyed by the anticipation of fresh bread and the stimulus of news and gossip. By dinner, however, as the temperature rose above eighty degrees in the cuddy, their spirits plummeted to join hers. Pangs of homesickness were sharpened by the increasing distance from the colony and the knowledge that at least six long weeks still stretched ahead before they arrived at their destination.

Finally, Henrietta was able to retire to her cabin to read Griffiths note. Having managed to stave off Hill's threat to take to the cabin with a liberal scrub of carbolic, she unfolded the note.

It was only one page of writing, enfolding a slip of paper no bigger than the tip of her finger with numbers written on it.

Dearest Henrietta,

Plans have gone awry, as plans do. You will have heard no doubt of Gipps' passing. I find gardening brings great solace. The water lily bulbs are all that will work to prevent the weeds. Here are the numbers of the seedlings you will need to plant, although they do need a lot of water. Keep yourself safe.

Your loving brother, Griff.

He was being careful, she knew, in case the letter fell into the wrong hands. But what did he mean by gardening? She was no gardener; Griffith knew that very well. There were beautiful water lilies in India, but she couldn't see how following that train of thought would help her discover his meaning.

She turned her attention to the slip of paper with the numbers. That was easier to decode. It could only be latitude and longitude. So, what was the location of the co-ordinates? She would have to find a way to enquire about it, from Mr Jackson perhaps. Mr Nash would be more easily duped, but less likely to be as competent as the first mate.

And why 'need a lot of water'? Dread enveloped her. Surely, she wasn't expected to pass on the documents at sea? It had been hard enough finding a way to collect them mid-voyage without drawing attention to herself. And who was she to hand them over to? Why couldn't she deliver them to someone in London? Or perhaps she should not bother with them at all. The situation had changed. Now, delivering them wouldn't benefit her in any way. It would only put her in danger; that is if Griffith's warning was to be believed.

She was still worrying at the puzzle when the clatter of children's footsteps told her that the dinner service for the adult passengers would start soon. She decided to keep the note with her at all times and stowed it in her bodice for safekeeping.

Captain Gallagher lumbered in to take his place at the table, his sun-weathered face ruddier than usual from the exercise of the day and the hospitality from the captain of the *Lenore*. Among the courses laid out, there was a large round of crusty baked bread, which sat beside an empty space reserved for the soup, its place marked by a ladle. The captain moved with deliberation, taking an inordinate amount of time as he drew his napkin up to his neck and tucked it into his collar.

The passengers were restive, but none more so than Lieutenant Gordon. Henrietta, seated beside him, caught a whiff of whiskey and wondered whose purchase he had been sharing.

Captain Gallagher cleared his throat and started to say grace. He articulated each word with care. By the time his tongue had navigated 'thankful', Lieutenant Gordon was fiddling with his spoon. Captain Gallagher frowned in aggravation but continued to say the final words.

The general amen was both prompt and heartfelt.

Lieutenant Gordon's hand shot forward, only to be pinned flat to the table by the captain's fist. The captain had leaned across the table with remarkable rapidity, given his previous slowness.

'What in damnation?' barked Lieutenant Gordon as he pulled his hand away.

'I'll remind you to mind your manners when grace is being said on board my ship. And your language too, if it comes to that. This is not the mess room, Lieutenant.'

The passengers stopped piling food on their plates. All eyes were on the captain.

John, the chief steward, headed out the door and tugged at James' sleeve to follow. James, however, stood transfixed, clutching at the well-worn serving cloth, which was all that preserved his fingers from the heat of the tureen full of steaming soup.

Lieutenant Gordon rose to his feet. 'And I'll have you know, I have not come on board a merchant ship to be taught manners.'

The sound of the wind and sea filled the silence. *So why are you on board*, Henrietta thought. And was it his failure to intercept the documents that was behind his drinking? Or perhaps, Gipps' death? Could he have hopes riding on Gipps' presence too? She heard the long honk of an albatross.

'So, Captain Gallagher, is it Trinidad or Tobago in the distance?' asked Miss McPhail to the surprise of all.

Distracted, the captain broke his glare at Lieutenant Gordon. But with a cry, James tripped and then, as the ship's motion shifted, he fell forward still gripping the tureen. The soup sloshed up the sides and spattered Henrietta as James attempted to compensate. Desperately, he landed the tureen on the table.

'Sorry, Lady Wood. So sorry,' he said with a gasp.

She waved him away, fearing he might try to wipe the spots on her dress with his grimy cloth. 'It's nothing, nothing at all.'

'Out,' shouted the captain.

Afterwards, Henrietta wondered if he had been shouting at James or Lieutenant Gordon, but in the event, it was James who left the cuddy. Perhaps Lieutenant Gordon had decided his hunger was greater than his dignity, although he remained silent for the rest of dinner.

At her second attempt, Miss McPhail directed her comment to the others. 'It's quite a coincidence that we saw two ships headed to Calcutta, isn't it? I thought their whole shipping industry had collapsed.'

This time she was more successful. The discussion of the financial woes of the East India Company lasted them until they'd finished eating. Mr Veitch held forth on the benefits of the Treaty of Nanking to Great Britain in ending the Canton system, and he argued that all that had been lost in India would be regained. Mr Quigley started up a long harangue on the evils of opium. Mrs Sapsford weighed in with the beautiful silks and other fabrics now available in Sydney, but the gentlemen ignored her.

Henrietta examined the spots where the soup had spattered her mauve gown. Such were the disadvantages of emerging from widow's black. And such were the disadvantages of not being able to afford a new dress without relying on the parsimonious support of one's relatives.

'The agency houses deserved everything they got, if you ask me,' intoned Mr Berkeley. 'They had it all, a complete monopoly, total control over shipping, and all they did was squander it—living like they were rajahs. They had their fingers in every pocket they could. Ships' captains were being convinced, coerced more like it, into contracts that made them think they owned their ships and their cargo. They were fooled into thinking they'd swing a deal for themselves in the selling. All along, the agencies were robbing them of their hard-earned money and paying them nothing for cargoes, blaming the European market on falling prices. And the partners of those firms—did they ever get prosecuted? Did they ever pay back what they owed?' He looked around, as if daring anyone to answer. 'No, no they didn't. They should have been pursued to the fullest extent of the law.'

The gentlemen murmured in a low rumble of agreement. Henrietta was still looking down at the stains on her dress, but she was not seeing the fabric.

Chapter 12

Nothing ventured, nothing gained

Henrietta

'Like to try your luck with a game of loo, Lady Wood?' suggested Mr Dempster. 'Mr Akers? Gordon? Mayhew?'

There was a noisy scraping of furniture as people rose from dinner. Henrietta, thankful for a distraction from her whirring thoughts about Griffith's message, drew the cards from a drawer in the sideboard.

Miss McPhail looked eager, but Mr Dempster said, 'Could I prevail on you for another drawing, Miss McPhail? You haven't done a portrait of me for my sister yet, and you do draw beautifully. You can sketch me while I'm playing. I'm sure Gordon would be happy to step in.'

Henrietta thought the number of members of Mr Dempster's family who required portraits seemed to grow with his preference for winning at cards. Miss McPhail was a shrewd player and regularly took the pot, while Lieutenant Gordon's playing was impetuous and unsuccessful.

The game proceeded quietly for a while, but on his third chance to win the trick, Mr Dempster turned over his card. It failed to trump Mr Mayhew's card.

'Put in your loo then, Dempster,' said Mr Mayhew.

'It was the wind from the skylight blowing the card over. Pass,' replied Mr Dempster.

Lieutenant Gordon, who was ahead in the game for once, looked at him grimly. 'Come on, pay up.'

Mr Akers took out his notebook. 'I can make a note, if you'd prefer?'

Mr Dempster threw his cards on the table. 'I said, pass. If you're going to accuse me of cheating, I'm out of the game.' He looked over at Miss McPhail. 'Finished yet?' Abandoning the game, he went over to sit beside her.

'Another game of loo, Mr Mayhew?' Henrietta asked uncertainly as Lieutenant Gordon shuffled the cards angrily.

Mr Dempster's apparent pique didn't concern her. She was more worried about Mr Mayhew, whose brow was furrowed. He rubbed his forehead and squinted against the light of the lamp, which hung over the table, swaying with the ship's roll. She hoped he wasn't ailing, just when she might need to call upon him again.

'Forgive me, Lady Wood,' he said, rising to his feet. 'A slight headache. I might take the air for a short while, if you'll excuse me.'

Lieutenant Gordon pushed the deck of cards toward Mr Akers. 'Looks like cards are over for the evening. Perhaps Mayhew has the right idea.'

Mr Dempster rose to follow him.

'It's a warm evening, and Trinidad in the sunset would be a sight to remember if you'd like to join us?' he said to Miss McPhail.

Mr Quigley and Mr Veitch frowned their disapproval over the top of their books. Mrs McPhail was settled in the corner of the side sofa, her head bent to her embroidery.

At Miss McPhail's imploring look, Henrietta said, 'That sounds like a delightful idea.'

Once on deck, Henrietta was pleased she had agreed to play chaperone. From the quarterdeck, she caught glimpses of the shiny backs of a school of porpoises as they gambolled alongside the ship. Mr Mayhew, Lieutenant Gordon and Mr Dempster had sought the poop deck for the higher vantage point. The sun was large and hovered above the far dark shape of an island in the distance.

'Lady Wood?' said Miss McPhail. 'Could I ask if—I mean, how did you know if you had met your future husband?' She glanced in the direction of the gentlemen as if fearful of being overheard.

Henrietta's eyebrows arched. 'Which one?' Taking pity on Miss McPhail's obvious discomposure, she continued, 'I was much younger than you when I made the acquaintance of my first husband, Mr Richeley. Patrick. It seems so silly to think of him as Mr Richeley when I think of how young we were.'

'So how could you be sure?'

'Well, it wasn't so much that I knew he was the right man for me to marry. It was more that I knew who I did not wish to marry.' She laughed at the startled look on Miss McPhail's face. 'I was young, and the young are always beautiful to the old. But to the young, even a modest gap in years can render the adult elderly. The old man who put his proposal to my uncle was among the richest men in Calcutta. No doubt my life would have been different had I accepted. My aunt was keen to get me off her hands. I saw it was a question of marrying or returning to my father's house in Sydney. But Patrick—well, Patrick was only eighteen when I first arrived to live with my uncle and aunt. Once my brother Griffith entered the Navy, Patrick and I spent a lot of time together. I thought him great fun. Well, he had nothing by way of fortune, of course, and Uncle Piggott took some persuading. In the end, he came around.'

'That doesn't seem very romantic, though.'

'Ah, romance. That's a different question.'

And a different person.

Unbidden memories of Baron de Bougainville swam before her—so handsome, so tall, so manly, such strong features and thick, wavy, black hair. Something niggled at the back of her mind, but she couldn't quite draw it out.

'I know what you must think, Lady Wood. I am well aware that lately my prospects have improved with the death of my father and the inheritance he bestowed upon me. But don't I have the right to ask for what any other woman might consider her due?'

Henrietta came back to the present moment. She thought that if Miss McPhail was waiting for romance, then that time had well and truly passed. 'What is it you want from life, Bridget?' she said. 'There is romance in situations, perhaps, rather than in people, don't you think?'

The soft tropical air around them reminded her of the languid hours seated on the veranda in Agra with Patrick. From there they could gaze across the river to the long-neglected Taj Mahal, the ruins of love for a dead wife.

'That's the same thing, isn't it? The man you marry and the life you live afterwards, I mean.' Miss McPhail's voice wobbled. 'How do you know what your life will be like after you've married?'

Henrietta realised the gentlemen had made their way down to the quarterdeck and were nearly within earshot. 'You'd never guess what Mr Richeley's first present to me after our marriage was—a lottery ticket. As you can imagine, I was none too impressed. A few days later, two young boys rushed into my drawing room, saying the "Lac of Rupee Prize" was mine.'

Miss McPhail gasped.

Henrietta smiled wryly. 'At that moment, Mr Richeley was out on business. When he arrived home, of course, he lost no time in going to ascertain the facts. Unfortunately, my ticket was one next to the prize. So you see—'

Mr Dempster must have caught some of the story. 'A sad tale indeed Lady Wood but, as they say, nothing ventured, nothing gained.'

'So, what do you think, Miss McPhail?' asked Lieutenant Gordon.

Miss McPhail started and then recovered herself as she saw Lieutenant Gordon's sweeping gesture to the horizon. 'Yes, quite lovely.'

'And so reassuring that the ship's chronometer is so accurate, don't you think, Mr Mayhew?' Henrietta said as he joined them by the rail. 'Would you be aware of today's latitude and longitude, perhaps?'

But Mr Mayhew was clearly following his own line of thought. 'I'm even more reassured by Mr Jackson's navigation skills, to tell the truth. If we were solely in our good captain's hands …'

Mr Mayhew left his sentence unfinished, as they heard Mrs Sapsford's voice calling to them from the cuddy. 'We're having a song, and I need Miss McPhail to assist,' she then said.

Henrietta followed along while they all dutifully trouped into the cuddy.

Did Mr Mayhew not keep track of their journey? She had seen him jotting down the latitude and longitude in his notebook. Perhaps if she asked him frankly? But that would mean explaining her secret, wouldn't it? She doubted she could involve him further without some explanation. Naturally, she could assume his patriotism, and this mission had—after all—been under the auspices of Governor Gipps originally.

Griffith's cryptic note had changed all that. He seemed to be telling her to hand over the documents while still at sea, and that suggested the information wouldn't be headed to London at all. So, then, would the documents be taken directly to France to warn King Louis Philippe? But public sentiment had shifted since the long and costly wars against Napoleon. She was sure that, if she were to ask, many of the passengers would say the British monarchy would do better to shore up its own support. Where would Mr Mayhew's sympathies lie?

Would she have a better chance if she asked Mr Jackson? The trouble was—Mr Jackson was not the sort of man susceptible to her charms. He kept himself apart, even when he joined them at dinner occasionally.

In the cuddy, Mr Akers had got out his fiddle and the company were in the midst of a rousing chorus. Mrs Sapsford convinced Miss McPhail to join her in a duet for 'Am I Not Fondly Thine Own'. Miss McPhail was able to keep a tune more accurately of the two of them but lacked confidence. Unfortunately, Mrs Sapsford lacked for nothing but an ear for music, and she then embarked on a solo performance of 'The Last Rose of Summer'. Mr Akers pleaded medical duties and left to lance young McPhail's boils.

With the singing over, Miss McPhail and Mr Dempster started up a game of écarté, and Mrs McPhail resumed her sewing. Mr Quigley and Mr Veitch buried their heads in their books, while Mr Berkeley and Mr Sapsford became immersed in a game of chess.

Mr Mayhew took up his copy of Alison's *History of Europe* but set it down on the table, rubbing his brow.

'Is your head still troublesome?' Henrietta asked. 'I have some attar if that might help.'

'No, no fakir remedies,' he said. 'Sorry, it is kind of you to offer. It will ease in its own time.'

Henrietta leaned across and picked up his book. 'Perhaps I could read to you, if you like?' She leafed through the pages. Seeing her opportunity, she turned to the Napoleonic wars. 'Is this the latest volume? I haven't had the chance to look at it yet. Fancy, Napoleon being written into history. It is odd, is it not, when things you remember get put into the history books?'

Mr Mayhew cleared his throat.

'Mr Mayhew wasn't even born when Napoleon fell, Lady Wood,' Mr Dempster said.

'I recall it only too well,' said Mrs McPhail, holding her needle with her arms extended at full length as she threaded it.

'There was nothing else in the paper for weeks,' said Mr Quigley. 'You remember, don't you, Mr Veitch?'

'I recall my parents talked a lot about it at the time, but I was too young to register the import,' said Mr Veitch.

Henrietta fought down her embarrassment. 'There was a great deal of fuss at the time, though I'm sure I was too young to read the newspapers. My father took us all into town and there was a Royal Salute from Dawes Battery. In the evening, there was a general illumination and it transformed Sydney into a kind of fairyland.'

In fact, her main memory of the outing was that she and Griffith had badgered her parents to let them walk about accompanied by the handsome Captain Cowin. She hadn't the courage to say more than two words to this Adonis before, but in the jostle of the streets, he'd told her more about his next posting to Ceylon.

A year later, in her adolescent geographical naivety, she had determined to follow him by taking up her aunt's invitation to visit Calcutta. It was his fault she had ended up in India. What would poor Bridget McPhail think of that romance?

With Mr Akers, Lieutenant Gordon rejoined them in a much-improved mood. As they talked on, it became clear their elevated spirits related to the whiskey, which Mr Akers had purchased from the *Lenore*. They drew up chairs and poured more of the moselle from dinner for Henrietta, Mrs McPhail and Mrs Sapsford.

After a loud tale from Mrs Sapsford about the dangers for ladies of falls in the days before the wearing of undergarments became fashionable, a grim-faced Mr Veitch said that Mrs Veitch would wonder where he was. He bade them goodnight and Mr Berkeley followed his example. Mr Quigley, too hard of hearing to catch the less than respectable conversation, remained immersed in his book.

Mrs McPhail, on the other hand, left her sewing aside and swayed in her seat with the roll of the ship. 'Didn't something of the sort happen to you, Lady Wood?' She suppressed a hiccough.

Henrietta looked at her, taken aback. *Is she referring to falling without undergarments on?*

Mrs McPhail went on and said, 'I mean, for some young ladies at some dinner or other for the judges? Wasn't it at Carter Lodge? Didn't I hear some tale about an incident in a loft, where ladies where "exposed"?'

Henrietta laughed, relieved to have caught the gist. 'I assure you the story is entirely apocryphal. The ceiling above did give way, but the young ladies in question were in fact fully clothed. Apart from a glimpse of their stockinged feet, the only harm done was a seasoning of plaster added to the mutton. Mr

Mayhew, I appeal to you. I'm sure Lady Ferris would have refuted that old story.'

Mr Mayhew smiled, his tense forehead relaxing for a moment. 'Aunt Clara rather enjoyed the telling of the tale, I have to say. Her account included some speculation as to what they were doing in the loft in the first place. However, in essentials, her story agrees with yours, Lady Wood.'

'Do have another, Mrs McPhail.' Lieutenant Gordon offered the bottle of whiskey this time. 'Any more secret tales you might like to tell us?'

Mrs McPhail moved forward a fraction to hold out her glass, but the wide eyes of her daughter brought her up short. 'Thank you, but perhaps not on this occasion. Spirits are a trifle too strong for me. But perhaps some more of the moselle?'

'What about you, Dempster?' Lieutenant Gordon was generous with Mr Akers' whiskey. 'Any secret tales? You're a man of secret handshakes, after all.'

'A freemason then, Mr Dempster?' Mrs McPhail asked.

To Henrietta, it appeared he hesitated to answer.

Mrs McPhail saved him as she continued, 'Mr McPhail was one, you know. All very mysterious.' She gave another hiccough. 'But it gave him something to do. Very useful for a gentleman to have some kind of occupation in the evenings.'

Henrietta said, 'I often tried to acquire some of their secrets. My first husband was one, of course, in Calcutta. I always wondered what they got up to at their meetings. One evening I found him trying to wash the carmine from off his eyebrows and fingernails, almost as if he were ashamed.'

'Nothing to be ashamed of.'

They all started. They had forgotten Mr Quigley was still with them.

He carried on saying, 'Freemasonry offers a social and spiritual fraternity. Never could see why the Catholics made such a fuss about it. Perfectly harmonious with the Christian faith.' With that pronouncement he subsided into his book.

Miss McPhail asked timidly, 'So, Mr Dempster, have you been a freemason long?'

Lieutenant Gordon spoke for him. 'Long enough to be bejewelled. I tell you, I've seen his apron.'

Mr Dempster's smile was forced, but he directed his attention to respond to Miss McPhail. 'I'm a past Master of St Paul's Lodge.'

Miss McPhail nodded, looking impressed.

John, the chief steward, started to clear the table with the brisk efficiency of one who'd finished waiting, and if they were not going to head to their cabins then that was no reason for him to delay his final duties for the evening. He avoided eye contact as if by that means he could obtain the requisite invisibility.

However, Lieutenant Gordon thwarted his efforts. 'I'll be keeping that,' he said, swiping his glass from the table. 'If Mr Akers starts drinking from the flask, there won't be a drop left for the rest of us.'

Mr Akers grasped the neck of the flask in mock possession. His eyes were puffy and half-closed. He scanned the room blearily. 'On your own, John? Why isn't your assistant here to give you a hand? Don't tell me James has been at the drink again?' His words were slurred.

John kept his gaze on the table. 'The captain's sent him forward to work as a sailor, Mr Akers. The soup at dinner was the last straw.'

'Doubt he'll make a much better sailor though,' said Mr Dempster. 'I'm sure James was a waiter at Petty's last time I was there.'

'He's a hard man, the captain,' said Lieutenant Gordon.

But Henrietta was tired of idle gossip. While they chattered, a whirlpool of great events was spinning around them, and it was she being sucked to the very centre. She stood and bad them goodnight.

The gentlemen rose as one, although Mr Akers' posture was more of a crouch performed while he held onto the table for balance. Henrietta thought it was as well cards were finished for the night—she doubted Mr Akers would be able to keep an accurate record of debts this evening.

Chapter 13

It would be churlish to refuse

Morgan

Morgan lay stiffly, fearful to move lest his migraine of the previous night shattered his head and sent a thousand stars exploding behind his eyes. His narrow cabin was dim and airless. His clothes from the previous night lay strewn on the floor where he left them. A plate with gravy covering a slab of mutton sat uneaten on the chest. It was so congealed that, even if it fell to the floor, he doubted whether the food would slide off. Last night, he had sent the stewards away when they enquired if he wanted Mr Akers to see to him, so at least he had been spared the application of leeches. He had enough experience of being bled during his childhood to know that such measures merely filled the time until the migraine cleared of its own accord.

The steward's hesitant knock broke his grey mood. Rolling over, he was relieved to find that only a dull ache lingered as the migraine slowly relinquished its grip. He pulled himself to a sitting position while James busied himself clearing away.

'Now, let me know if you feel an itch, Mr Mayhew. The Owens' children have still got head lice, and it doesn't take much for them to take off in a small space.

You ought to hear Mrs Sapsford on the subject. We've boiled everything they've touched and rubbed their heads with mutton fat and combed the critters out. If that doesn't work, Mrs Sapsford is threatening to shave their heads,' James explained.

'What's the weather like?'

'Very fine. The captain has invited the gentlemen to join him for some shooting, if you're up to it.'

Morgan stood, testing the effect on his head. 'Well, the worst seems to be over, so yes—shooting it is.'

Lady Wood raised her eyebrows when she caught sight of the gun. 'Shooting, Mr Mayhew? I was led to understand you had a headache?'

'A breath of fresh air,' he said, not stopping to talk. He felt that he had spent the entire voyage defending his actions against the teasing of Lady Wood.

On deck, Morgan saw Biggs, the midshipman, slumped against a pole. It took a moment to realise the man was bound with rope.

'Found his way down the hatchway last night to the stores and got well and truly drunk,' said Gordon. 'Kept trying to throw himself overboard, so the captain had him lashed to the pole. For his own safety, he says.'

'Enough chat, you two,' called Mr Dempster. 'I've got a pound that says my count will be higher than yours.' Mr Dempster was standing, sighting his rifle into the air.

The explosion sent a rolling wave of concussions through Morgan's head. A second later, and there was a thud of the bird hitting the deck. When he came to inspect the kill, it was an albatross. Mr Dempster tossed it casually onto a pile of mangled feathers.

'Didn't Coleridge have something to say on the subject?' asked Morgan.

'Stuff and nonsense, what would a poet know about it?' said Captain Gallagher. 'Sailors eat any bird they can kill, and albatross are fair game.' He took aim. 'That Cape Pigeon, there,' he said, firing.

The bird plummeted down into the sea.

'That's five to me, Mr Dempster. I think there'll be another entry in Mr Akers' ledger tonight.'

'Not shooting, Gordon?' Morgan asked, seeing that Gordon was not carrying his rifle.

'Not today,' he said airily. 'Miss McPhail and I have a game of chess to play, and she tells me she detests like the smell of shot.'

Mr Dempster's back stiffened, and he swung his gun high and fired. Nothing fell. 'Just missed,' he said under his breath.

They heard a stream of abusive language coming up from the lower deck.

'I see the good midshipman is awake,' Gordon said with a laugh.

'Enough, I tell you,' roared the captain, so close to Morgan's ear that he jumped. 'If he's not careful, I'll be using him for target practice.'

Biggs subsided.

'Are you shooting, Mayhew? Or standing there with your gun to show off for the ladies?' said Mr Dempster.

Morgan realised for the first time that they had an audience. Miss McPhail stood with her mother and brother. Joseph McPhail was giving a running commentary on the faults of the respective shooters. Mrs Sapsford and Mrs Berkeley had left the children to the servants and were watching with interest. And Lady Wood had returned, of course.

'Shooting,' Morgan replied. 'What's the bet again?'

'What do you think, Captain Gallagher?' asked Mr Dempster, narrowing his eyes speculatively. 'I'd put five shillings on Mayhew not getting more than one.'

The captain considered for a moment, taking in the ease with which Morgan carried his gun. 'Done.'

'Up to you whether you want to throw your money away, Mr Dempster,' said Morgan. 'You're on.'

By the end, his ears rang and his head pleaded for mercy. But he had added four more albatross to the pile, and Mr Dempster was the poorer for it. Poor Biggs was untied and told he was lucky to have avoided the lash. Gordon must have mentioned several times that he was heading to play his game of chess with Miss McPhail, before he went down to the cuddy.

Mr Dempster and Morgan sat side by side on the deck, cleaning their guns. The skies were bright and a fresh breeze was picking up. Morgan felt his head clear. Perhaps the shooting had blasted the last remnants of pain away.

'Damn Gordon,' said Mr Dempster. 'You don't think Miss McPhail can really be interested in him, do you? I mean, the man's got no prospects at all. From what I know about him, the only welcome he'll get when we land is a bailiff.'

'I doubt if he's told Miss McPhail such details,' said Morgan. He suspected Mr Dempster of similarly editing his personal finances.

'She's beguilingly innocent, really,' said Mr Dempster. 'I mean, she's not what you'd call young, but she has quite an appealing naivety.'

'So, you are fond of her?'

'Of course,' protested Mr Dempster. 'What do you take me for? Some kind of cad?'

Morgan was not going to answer that. Instead, he said, 'You want to clarify your intentions, that's all.'

'My intentions are perfectly honourable.'

'Old Quigley and Mr Veitch might disagree.'

'Well, you are the pot calling the kettle black, if you don't mind me saying,' he said. 'I could tell a tale or too about you and the ladies. I'm looking forward to telling your Miss Butler all about that ball at the governor's when you and Miss—' He left his sentence unfinished, seeing Lady Wood approach.

There was something in the way Lady Wood was looking at him that made him intensely uncomfortable. He had the feeling he was about to find himself doing something he didn't wish to. The hair-raising excursion in the jolly-boat was surely enough gallantry for one voyage, wasn't it? His stomach murmured queasily at the memory.

As the other passengers drifted away, he knew she would choose that moment to speak.

'Mr Mayhew, I wonder if I might impose on your goodwill again.' Catching his look, she hurriedly added, 'Not another adventure.'

The tinkle of her laughter suggested that to have thought otherwise of his trip in the jolly-boat was risible.

'The packet you passed on to me. Hill is intent upon scrubbing every inch of our cabin, and I'm wondering if you might look after it for me. Only for a short while? Oh, and just one other little packet too,' she asked.

Morgan's unease grew. He'd grown to manhood in a household of women. His sister and aunts could have matched Lady Wood in feminine wiles. 'If I'm to take possession of the packet, Lady Wood—'

'Only for a day, possibly less—'

'Then can you tell me the nature of the contents? In general terms, you understand. I have no wish to pry.'

Lady Wood avoided his eye. 'It is nothing of significance. Mementos that my brother wishes me to pass on to the family members I plan to visit in Kent. But they are of sentimental value. I would not want them to get wet.'

Morgan didn't believe a word of it.

On the face of it, her request was entirely reasonable. It would be churlish to refuse. As a green young man fresh off the boat, he would have been pleased to do anything Lady Wood asked. He would have even felt flattered to be asked.

But now?

Since he'd been in the colony, he'd been lied to, short-changed, conned, tricked and taken advantage of on a regular basis. If he had anything to be proud of among all the failures, it was that he'd come through with his own integrity intact.

'I'm so sorry, Lady Wood,' he said, formulating his response carefully. 'I find that on this occasion I can't be of assistance. I've asked the stewards to clean out my own cabin in the very same way.'

Her face betrayed her surprise, rapidly replaced with knowing anger. They both knew the game they were playing.

'Anyone for chess?'

At Gordon's voice, they started.

How long was he behind us?

'I've been beaten fair and square by Miss McPhail,' Gordon continued. 'I need to repair my confidence. Lady Wood?'

But Lady Wood excused herself abruptly. Whether her haste related to her anger with him or to a distaste for chess, Morgan didn't know.

Chapter 14

The water lily bulbs

Henrietta

Trying to ease the cramps gnawing her lower abdomen, Henrietta lay on her bunk. Her hands rested across her stomach as if by the pressure of her fingers she could soothe the dull aches beneath. It was over a year since the last time, and she and Hill had decided there would be no need to pack the usual paraphernalia. Hill, of course, was thoroughly disgruntled and behaved as if Henrietta was in some way responsible for the flood of blood. To give Hill her due, she sacrificed her own second-best petticoat for the rags they needed. Henrietta took another sip of tea but it had grown cold. Hill was avoiding coming in to check on her, so the likelihood of a fresh cup was low. Henrietta turned on her side.

After a few seconds, her eyes refused to stay closed. Not a breath of air came through from outside—the ship was barely moving, and the heat was oppressive. She rolled on her back again, becalmed. Cut off from companionship, she floated like some bloated whale carcass, neither coming nor going.

Mr Mayhew's refusal to take the documents for safekeeping disturbed her. He laughed at her funny tales and showed deference at every opportunity. She thought she had him in the palm of her hand. But, she hated to admit it to herself, his attentions were those due to a grande dame entering her senior years — a kind of flattery for what once had been. At her age, she was easy to refuse.

But that left her ill equipped to carry out any part of her mission. How could she inveigle Lord Grey into taking sympathy on her petition? How could she get the help she needed to ensure she made the mid-ocean rendezvous and hand over her documents?

She exhaled slowly, trying to release a wave of cramping. She fought the urge to curl into a ball. Instead, she arched her back to stretch and strain against the pain.

It seemed cruel that in later life she should feel the pains of womanhood when through her youth she had been so free of such cares. The first time was shortly before her father returned from his long four-year absence. She had been startled by the blood but not unduly troubled. The household at Aylesford had been so female while he was away in England for Johnston's court martial; the whole thing seemed perfectly natural and ordinary. Of course, that changed after his return — her mother tensely scolding her for mentioning it in her father's presence.

He died two years ago. While his death brought a resolution of sorts, she often had trouble believing he was gone. His belligerent voice chastised her in her mind. It had taken all her forgiveness to attend his deathbed …

Her carriage wound its way past the low-lying saltpans and turned into the estate. Once past the limekiln and the flour mill, Aylesford House came into view. The carriage halted in front of the steps to the house. The columns spoke of regency grandeur, but the upper floor formed a colonial veranda in the centre.

She stood for a moment, drinking in the manicured gardens and the glimpses of the Parramatta River flowing around the small promontory. The chapel had been new when she visited last, six years before, but its stark plainness had settled in among the trees. Would they bury her father beside it?

'Henrietta, what took you so long? Your father has been asking for you.'

Mama's tall figure approached from the gloom of the hallway, assisted by her maidservant.

So then, he's not dead yet. Henrietta suppressed a sigh.

She followed them back through the house—her mother navigated the stairs with considerable difficulty. Griffith had told her about her mother's illness, but it was a shock all the same. The once graceful Henrietta de Perroquet Burbridge struggled to move her left leg and arm. Her handsome face twisted with the palsy.

How had Beth coped? Why hadn't she called for her to see him earlier? But she knew the answer. The real question was: would he see her now?

Beth stood as they entered father's room. 'Mama, you should not have troubled yourself. The stairs are too much for you.' She looked sternly at Henrietta and added, 'Papa has been asking for you.'

The curtains were closed and, apart from a single oil lamp, the only light was from the fire, lit against the last of the winter's chill. The room was hot and close, and the smell was that blend of bodily miseries peculiar to the sick bed. Beth hurried to assist Mary to lead their mother back to her room to rest.

As Henrietta's eyes grew accustomed to the gloom, she made out Sutton, her father's manservant, standing to the side. Her first impulse was to tell him to open the curtains and let in some air, but the thought of Beth's reaction stopped her. She was determined to avoid any unnecessary friction. It was too long since she had been on speaking terms with any of them.

Instead, she sat in the chair that Beth had vacated beside the bed and looked at her father. The flesh from his stocky build had shrunk so that the folds of skin around his face and neck collapsed in on themselves. His remaining hair was thin and matted with sweat, and his eyes were closed in defeat.

'Henrietta,' he said.

'Mama has only just this minute left, Papa. Shall I get her for you?' She considered holding his hand but thought better of it.

'No, no.' His whisper took on the edge of his usual growl. 'Henrietta, Henrietta should be here. Don't tell me she's taken herself off to India again.'

Henrietta fought down her anger. He's dying, remember, he's dying. 'Papa, it's me, Henrietta. I've come.' She leaned forward and touched his forehead. His skin felt clammy.

His eyes opened and he stared at her intently. 'Yes, yes. So you are. That fool of a husband with you?'

She wondered which husband he meant. 'No, remember, Sir Giles passed on two years ago.'

He grunted. 'Didn't leave you anything, did he? Same as that jumped-up clerk in India. How does a man like that—?' He broke off, coughing. It was a weak, desperate cough.

Henrietta filled a cup with water from the pitcher by his bed and held his head up as he tried to drink.

'How does such a man think he can advise me?' her father rasped. 'I built this estate without any help from the likes of him. Another interfering government employee when all is said and done—the governors, the chief justices, the lot of them. What do they know about business?' He coughed again and, exhausted, he closed his eyes.

Henrietta sat, waiting for him to speak. *You must always wait in a conversation with Papa.*

Those who didn't know him well would take him to be finished and attempt to make some contribution. But, no sooner had they done so, he would start again regardless. Henrietta and Griffith used to amuse themselves by counting the seconds during his pauses. Griffith claimed the longest was thirty seconds, but Henrietta disputed his claim, since Papa had changed topic.

As she stared at his hands clasped on his chest, rising imperceptibly with each shallow breath, she reached thirty-five. She must remember to tell Griffith.

'So, if you think to come here and curry favour then you're much mistaken, my girl.' He went on, eyes still closed. 'I don't owe you a penny. You're as profligate as Griffith. It was a mistake to let you two head off for India so young. But your mother was set on it. She was always filling your head with nonsense about maharajahs and elephants, as if it would all be the same as her childhood memories of the place. If I'd had my way, things would have been very different. You both had every opportunity. But if it hadn't been for me, neither of you would have had a roof over your head after Richeley died.'

She closed her eyes.

He had been silent for a while, and she had forgotten to count. She checked his clasped hands across his chest and saw them rise and fall.

Later, Mary came to assist Sutton to prepare her father for the night. Henrietta joined Beth, who was making a sketch of a dried flower—flattened from its time under the heavy weight of books.

Beth glanced up from her drawing, her stick of charcoal pressed to the paper. 'Mama will have a tray taken to her room. She shouldn't have over-exerted herself coming downstairs to greet you.' The charcoal snapped. 'Over the last few weeks, we have been having a light supper in here of an evening. It seems silly to sit in the dining room with only the two of us.'

'Yes, very sensible,' Harried replied. She sat at the piano and her fingers found their way over the familiar keys.

Beth looked tired. When Henrietta had last seen her younger sister, she had already joined her sister Rose in the ranks of the spinsters at balls and parties. It was absurd they had stayed unmarried in a colony with twice as many men as women, but no suitor met their mother's hopes or their father's expectations. At thirty-eight years of age, the lines on Beth's brow were etched permanently. Her round face resembled Rose's, but without her doe-eyed softness. The Misses Burbridge were welcome wherever they went, such good company, so amenable. Such good daughters to their ageing parents.

Henrietta's own face, in contrast, owed more to her mother's strong features. The reflection in the polished wood of the piano reassured her—forty-five and not a wrinkle.

Beth rubbed at her blackened fingers with a rag. 'Well then? What did he need to see you about so urgently?'

'I have no idea, unless it was to take one last opportunity to berate me.'

The corner of Beth's mouth twitched. 'I have been thinking his anger is keeping him alive. Mama is the only one who can settle him down. Every little thing sets him off. All the old matters.'

'Don't tell me—Banks deceived him, he was promised more land, more men. Bligh was an oppressor with no regard for the law. Macquarie, Brisbane, Darling, Bourke, Gipps—none of the governors were more than time-serving puppets of the Colonial Office waiting for their cosy government pensions.'

Beth's smile broke through. 'Don't forget the Chief Justice.'

Henrietta laughed. 'Yes, I was just reminded of Sir Giles' temerity. How dare he give William Burbridge, Esquire, advice regarding his legal obligations?'

When their supper arrived, they ate companionably.

'I was sorry Papa forbade you from coming to see me after we heard Rose had died,' said Beth.

Her mother had sustained the estrangement, but the family always spoke as if Papa had the final word in the household.

But even if this had not been the case, she would have found it difficult to convince Sir Giles to let her visit. He was outraged by her father's accusations that his advice constituted dishonourable interference. He felt the prohibition of any of the family to see him or Henrietta even more keenly than she had.

By the time they heard from England of Rose's death, Sir Giles was ill himself. It all seemed so pointless, all the anger and recriminations. She could see no point in pursuing it.

'Has Griffith been?' she asked.

'Yes, but he didn't stay long. Papa got so agitated, Mama was worried.'

'He's not still harping on about the money Griffith owes him, surely?'

Beth evidently took the question as rhetorical, since she went back to her sketch without answering.

Henrietta volunteered to sit by her father for much of the night—at least he kept his silence when sleeping, and she was generous with the laudanum.

If she had thought her vigil would soften her mother's attitude, then she was mistaken. The next morning, as Henrietta drooped with fatigue over the breakfast table, her mother patted Beth on the arm.

'You're looking weary, dearest. Perhaps you could have a nap this morning, now Henrietta has come.' Her mother's intonation implied Henrietta had stayed away wilfully.

'No, no. Papa will want me to read to him,' Beth answered.

'You're an angel, dear. He does love it when you read.'

Henrietta had hoped she might catch up on some sleep while Beth was with her father, but her mother insisted on her company. She looked through the bookshelf for some distraction. Her hand fell on *The Felonry of New South Wales*. 'I'm amazed this is allowed in the house,' she said.

'Edward and Arthur purchased a copy in order to prepare their retort,' her mother said. 'I'm disappointed that you have the indelicacy to look at it, now of all times.'

Henrietta took the book to her seat. 'I was busy when it came out—what with the preparations for Elizabeth's wedding.'

Her mother sniffed. 'Your father should have sued the blackguard. I told him so at the time.'

'What for saying?' She began to read aloud. 'Mr Burbridge—certainly a very worthy and reputable, as well as a portly and good-natured man—was originally a yeoman in the county of Kent.'

The steel in her mother's eye told her she knew what she was up to. She closed the book but kept her finger between the pages to mark the spot. It had always been one of her favourite sections of the book. *But the idea of making this English yeoman—this worthy 'man of Kent' —a legislator is as preposterous as it would be to make him archbishop of Australia, or poet laureate to his Excellency Governor Bourke.* 'Ah well, there were a lot of people in the colony who wanted to sue Mr Mudie,' she said. 'Did Mr Kinchela ever win his case?'

Her mother pursed her lips.

Henrietta continued to leaf through the book and the silence between them deepened. She knew her mother would break it. She was too talkative a woman to stay quiet long.

'Papa and I were most sorry to learn of Sir Giles' passing,' her mother said stiffly. 'I hear you are comfortably relocated.'

Henrietta assumed Griffith must have described the small cottage that Edmund Wood had arranged for her while Carter Lodge was let to pay the creditors.

'You heard about poor Rose, I suppose?' her mother asked. Her mother always referred to 'poor Rose' when talking about her with Henrietta, in much the same way as she would refer to 'dearest Beth'.

Henrietta nodded.

'So sad for poor Rose to die so far from us all—'

And unmarried, thought Henrietta.

'And unmarried,' finished her mother.

Henrietta lowered her gaze in an effort to look contrite. But her lids were heavy and began to close.

Her mother continued, 'It's not that she didn't have her chances, such a pretty girl, such gentle features. Baron de Bougainville was quite taken with her that day at the picnic, you remember. Until you decided to throw yourself at him—and you, a married woman ...'

Her memories of de Bougainville had kept her awake through her mother's well-worn tirade, which continued for some time—she had covered ten years of Henrietta's life.

'And Rose could have been Lady Wood. All through her illness, dear Mary urged Sir Giles to marry again. He proposed first to Rose, you know.'

Yes, Henrietta did know ...

Feeling the cramping ease, she struggled to sit. She decided to change the cloth pad. Hill would complain about yet another to rinse and dry—but the pad was rank in the heat. A quick wash made her feel almost human, and she placed a cool damp cloth around her neck and reached for her fan.

She sat, becalmed as the ship. If only it would move. Somewhere ahead, a ship prowled the shipping lanes waiting for the *Lord Henderson*. Waiting for her to drop the documents to the other ship—but what ship? She drew Griffith's note out from her bodice and mulled over his message, yet again.

The water lily bulbs are all that will work to prevent the weeds. Here are the numbers of the seedlings you will need to plant, although they do need a lot of water.

With absolute clarity she saw the water lilies in her mind's eye.

Hyacinths.

Finally, her mind let her see the connection.

What would her life have been if she'd fled with Baron Hyacinthe de Bougainville? The French were more liberal about such things, of course, but all the same … She wished she were with him now. But his death had been reported in the papers only last year. He would have known what to do about the secret documents, she was sure. He might even have sailed out in *L'Ésperance* and leapt aboard and whisked both her and the documents away as the loyal royalist he had been.

But Griffith knew of his death, so why allude to him?

Slowly, she understood. Griffith could only mean that it would be the French royalists, not the British, who would pick up the documents. From what she'd already gleaned from Mr Nash, the ship's course would take them closer to France than England for some distance.

She traced the lines around her neck. She was now the same age de Bougainville had been when they'd met twenty years ago. She might be an ageing grande dame, but perhaps she should try to obtain the assistance of the first mate. Yes, she told herself, and Mr Jackson would be likely to be of far more help than Mr Mayhew in reaching the drop-off point.

There was a soft tap on the cabin door. *Too gentle to be Hill.*

'I've been worrying you've been unwell, Lady Wood. I do hope you'll excuse me for visiting uninvited.' Mrs McPhail bustled her way into the cabin.

'Not at all, do come in,' Henrietta said through gritted teeth. Now she had decided upon Mr Jackson, she was determined to seek out an opportunity to talk with him immediately.

'We've all missed you, you know. Things are not nearly so lively without you. All the gentlemen say so.'

Itching with irritation, Henrietta assumed from the way Mrs McPhail twisted her handkerchief that she couldn't suppress the reason for the visit much longer.

'I married Mr McPhail when I was very young, you know,' she blurted.

Henrietta waited in silence for her to continue. Sometimes with Mrs McPhail, interruptions could lead to lengthy detours, which was best avoided.

'And so I do not have your, your experience, if I can use that word, of the world. I think that Mr Dempster

may have some notions with respect of my Bridget,'
Mrs McPhail said.

'Yes, indeed,' Henrietta said, speedily. Though the
question was really: what kind of intentions.

'But Mr Quigley has had a quiet word to me and
suggested, oh—' Mrs McPhail seemed overcome.

'What, that Bridget should be less, forthcoming?'
Henrietta rather thought that Miss McPhail might be
better advised to use every charm she had available,
however slight, if she wanted to secure a match.

'Yes, yes, that's it.'

'I'm not sure if it helps, Mrs McPhail, but when I
married for the second time, I was about your Bridget's
age.'

Mrs McPhail flinched at the acknowledgement of
her daughter's long spinsterhood.

'Sir Giles' wife, Mary, had been unwell for some
time. She was a good friend of my mother's, you know.
Well, as it became clear the end would be soon, Mary
drew me aside to confide that she had begged Sir Giles
to promise to marry again, for the children's sake.'

'Poor Sir Giles,' said Mrs McPhail.

'Well, what could I do? What should I do? If a
woman stands back too far then she risks being
overlooked.'

'Do you think so?' asked Mrs McPhail, her
furrowed brow relaxing.

Good, thought Henrietta. Her mind was buzzing. Time to talk with Mr Jackson about the coordinates. They must be close. And perhaps she should get him to ensure that a bucket was left on deck. She might have to lower the packet of documents overboard in the bucket. But how could she manage to do that without being seen by the sailors on watch? It would have to be at night. And it would help if there were fewer sailors too.

Chapter 15

A nasty sting

Morgan

Morgan woke, momentarily disoriented. There was that rustle again. Repeatedly, through the howling winds and seas of the night before, the sound had managed to find its way into his fitful sleep. The wind had abated, but the ship continued to heave its way through the swell. He reluctantly opened his eyes, peering about in the early morning gloom of his cabin while the rustling gave way to a scrabbling. *Not rats, please, not rats.*

He swung his legs over the side of his bunk, reaching across to the drawers to dress, steadying himself against the lurching motion of the ship with the other hand.

The drawer was barely three inches open when a furred ball wriggled through and launched itself onto the floor, claws catching in the rough weave of the blankets he had thrown from his bunk in the warmth of the night. In the seconds it took to extricate its claws and scurry to the false safety of the narrow space between the boxes under his bunk, Morgan made out the light fur of its underbelly and the white spots blotched across its back.

He cursed under his breath—one of the native cats the captain had brought on board.

He rapidly finished dressing and headed out in search of the steward, his arms outstretched to maintain his balance. At the steps leading up to the deck, he found the first mate on his way down after finishing his watch.

'One of the damn native cats is loose, Jackson. You'd better let the captain know.' He flushed. It wasn't fair to swear at Jackson over it.

Mr Jackson didn't seem to have taken offence. 'Blast him. He lets the damn things run about his cabin. He reckons to tame the things by the end of the voyage. One of the pests killed all my budgerigars even before we left Sydney. I'll get the blacks onto it.'

Within seconds, he was back followed closely behind by the lean figures of Tommy and Jimmy.

Morgan and Jackson stayed in the passageway peering into the cabin while Tommy knelt to catch sight of the animal cowering in the far corner under the bunk. After a rapid exchange in their own language, Jimmy took the blanket from the floor and laid it out as if it were a net, two corners grasped in each hand. He crouched, ready to draw it together when the moment came.

Tommy pulled off his knotted rope belt and, keeping hold of one end, shallow cast the belt out under the bed in the direction of the cat. Then he wriggled the belt so it snaked as he drew it back towards him. On the third try, the native cat pursued it, only to find itself caught in the makeshift net and hoisted into the tight grip of Jimmy, now standing upright and laughing with Tommy, who was recapturing his fallen trousers with the woven belt.

Morgan found himself alone in the cuddy for breakfast. It was the third morning where seasickness had almost universally immobilised the passengers. Most made their way on deck where they gazed fixedly at the horizon in the determined effort to quell the nausea.

Not Lady Wood, however, who had remained below for days.

Why had her manner changed towards him? Could she really have been so put out by his refusal to take charge of that packet? Or perhaps she thought their age difference made their friendship unsuitable? Why hadn't he been able to find some way to move past the awkwardness of her inclusion of him in recollections of Napoleonic times?

He flinched again to think of it. But he was no courtier, surely she knew that.

He shook the thoughts away. She had been unwell. He'd heard that her poor burned fingers had been bound in gauze. Fool of a steward, letting her try to relight a hot lantern.

'You have an exceptionally strong stomach, Mr Mayhew.'

Lady Wood gracefully manoeuvred her way into the cuddy and to the table while holding onto the furniture for balance.

'And you are quite recovered, Lady Wood?' He glanced at her gloved hands.

'Yes, I have paid my penance for impatience and in recognition have been given a reprieve from mal de mer, for which I am truly thankful.' She eyed the dish of devilled kidneys near her dubiously. 'Though perhaps bread would be sufficient for the moment.'

'The punishment does not seem to have matched the offence though, if I may be the judge. After all, the lantern did not suffer as you did.'

'That is kind of you. I shall consider myself fortunate that my ill-judged actions only affected a lantern, which can only wreak a small penalty.' Lady Wood nibbled gingerly on a piece of dry bread. 'It puts me in mind of a story I once heard.'

Morgan smiled and nodded, relieved Lady Wood appeared to have completely forgotten or forgiven his lack of assistance.

'Well, as I'm sure a gentleman so well versed in the study of Natural History.' She then went on. 'You will know the intelligence of an elephant can be hardly overrated, besides their keen sense of justice. You may know of Sir David Ochterlony?' She didn't pause for a reply. 'In India, I had the honour of an invitation to visit him during his time as Resident Commissioner of Delhi. I have this story from his lips, and he was a man who knew a great deal about elephants.'

'Did you …?' Morgan wanted to ask her if she had met any of the thirteen concubines he was rumoured to promenade with every evening, each perched on an elephant, but was having difficulty thinking of how to put such a question delicately.

Lady Wood's eyebrows arched even higher by way of answering before she proceeded. 'Sir David told me about a mahout who on several occasions had withheld the full number of loaves of bread allowed his elephant, upon which the animal expressed his anger by refusing to eat any. Repeated instances of the same mistreatment at length provoked resentment in the elephant until he was beyond control, and he crushed the man to death under his knees.'

Morgan went to speak, but Lady Wood continued, 'The son of the mahout, only nine years of age, was standing there screaming when it happened. The elephant gently twined his trunk round the boy's waist and placed him on his neck, and never from that time suffered anyone else to attend upon him.' She paused for effect. 'I think the elephant must have felt sorry for what he had done, but Sir David was of the opinion that, justice having been served, the elephant was making sure he had an obedient master.'

Morgan laughed. 'No doubt that tells us much about the differences between yourself and Sir David Ochterlony.'

Lady Wood smiled appreciatively, and Morgan relaxed for the first time in days, basking in the glow of her expression.

After a second cup of tea, their conversation turned to their fellow passengers.

'And has anyone seen Mrs Veitch?' she asked.

'She has become quite a mystery to us all,' he replied. 'I did see her as we boarded, of course, but I have barely laid eyes on her since. However, Mr Veitch keeps her in our thoughts with constant reminders of opinions he has shared with her.'

'Perhaps I should visit. What do you think? The poor woman has been seasick for the entire voyage.' She sounded tentative.

'Mm. Mrs Sapsford has intimated that Mrs Veitch's infirmity may relate to something other than seasickness.' Morgan said. *Is Lady Wood asking if I have heard the rumours of Mrs Veitch's drinking problem?*

'No, on this occasion I think Mrs Sapsford is mistaken,' Lady Wood said.. 'I am more concerned about the effects of Mr Veitch's drinking on her health.'

Morgan was mystified.

'Men who drink in private often, in my experience,' she said, 'can be a danger to their families. Not every elephant rebels against their mahout.'

'Well, I gather none of the other ladies have visited her yet,' he said, not wishing to be drawn into her speculation. 'Mrs Veitch might enjoy the company of someone other than her husband for a while.'

'No doubt that is good advice, Mr Mayhew.' Lady Wood seemed about to go on, but they were interrupted by the chattering entry of the Berkeley children, with old Mr Quigley making his way arthritically to his seat.

Morgan fought down his irritation at the abrupt end to their conversation. Why was it that the young and the old had such surprising resilience?

Lady Wood, as usual, began to chat merrily with the children.

Morgan tried to recapture her attention. 'One of the captain's native cats found its way into my cabin last night.'

Thirteen-year-old Charley looked excited. 'Did it bite you?'

'Oh no,' cried his sister Adelaide. 'Had it been anywhere else? Did it eat any of the birds? Have they caught it? Where is it?'

As the younger children started to pay attention, Morgan regretted introducing the topic. It only struck him as he spoke that he was not at all sure what had happened to the cat. Mr Jackson's growl of 'Now to put you where you belong' was ominous.

Anxious to end the conversation, he said, 'I'll just go and check on my birds.'

As Morgan got to his feet, Mr Quigley said, keeping his voice down so as not to be overheard, 'I'm not entirely sure, but I was up on deck only a moment ago, and I think I saw one of the blacks tossing some kind of animal overboard. Perhaps it was whatever was in your cabin. Do you think I should tell the captain?'

Thinking furiously, Morgan said, 'The captain will have just come off his watch. I doubt if he'd thank you for waking him. You might have a word with Mr Jackson though.'

Mr Quigley nodded thoughtfully, blowing on his porridge.

To his surprise, Lady Wood gently ejected the youngest Berkeley from her lap and stood to join him. 'So, Mr Mayhew,' she murmured. 'It was as well I didn't hand over my documents for your safekeeping. Your cabin turned out not to be the sanctuary I anticipated.'

Morgan lent his arm to assist her balance as they left, aware Lady Wood had certainly not forgotten his lack of assistance and knowing he had been chastised, albeit gently.

In the stern of the ship, Morgan felt the rebellion of his recently eaten breakfast. In the warmth, the smell from the animals reached a foul retching pungency. His grasp on the cages tightened as he fought for control.

Lady Wood's face was pale in the gloom.

Together, they peered into the cages holding his budgerigars and found another four lying dead on the floor of the cage.

'Were you planning to sell them?' asked Lady Wood, one hand resting on the cage, the other on his arm—whether in sympathy or for balance, he couldn't tell.

He shook his head. 'No, well not all of them. I remember Lucy telling me about the beautiful humming birds she used to see as a child in Jamaica. I wanted to give these to show her something of the beauty in her future home.'

They moved on, stepping carefully as the ship rose and fell, until they came to the cages of parrots belonging to Lady Wood. Even in the dim light, their plumage flashed vivid red, bright green and brilliant blue as they hopped and fluttered across the perches.

'Rainbow lorikeets,' Lady Wood said authoritatively.

They stood watching in silence for a while.

'I wonder what they think as we stare in at them in their cages,' said Morgan.

'We'll be a bit like them, you know, back home,' said Lady Wood. 'When in Calcutta, I felt like I was some kind of bird in a cage. All the fussing and comments—"Ooh, the Botany Bay Flower".' She adopted a mock disapproving tone and continued, '"And she has such a high colour", and when I spoke up or laughed or danced then "she has such delightful natural high spirits". Even in another colony, you'll always be a "colonial" being stared at.'

'But I'm going home, to people I know well,' he said.

'Is it still your home?' she asked. 'It's been seven years. They'll have changed while you've been gone.'

He thought of Lucy and realised for the first time that he had no idea what she might look like, transformed from a girl to a woman. 'But I haven't changed.'

'You think not? I remember seeing you when you first arrived. You remember that dinner the Ferris gave for you and your sister?'

He nodded, the memory of meeting her blanched from his recall in the tidal wash of the new sights and experiences of Sydney. He remembered he had thought her old then, just the mother of her far more interesting household of young adult children and stepchildren around his own age.

She continued relentlessly, 'How different you are from that unworldly youth.'

He saw her gaze marking his tanned face, the width of his shoulders and his roughened hands still clasping the cage, although there was no need—the sea had finally begun to settle to an even rhythm. He looked away sharply. 'But is it *your* home? You haven't been back since you were six.'

She stood very still and for one awful moment he thought her friendship lost to him. But then she smiled ruefully, and he felt her hand rest lightly on his.

'No, no doubt I shall be a parrot in a cage. But after a while, perhaps they will mistake this parrot for a robin.'

'Mr Mayhew, Mr Mayhew, Lady Wood, Lady Wood,' came the loud cries of Charley Berkeley, the clatter of his footsteps coming toward them.

Lady Wood was the first to react. 'What's wrong, Charley?' she called as she stepped away from the cages.

'Sharks, Lady Wood. Sharks everywhere. Come and see, Mr Mayhew.' Charley Berkeley was so excited he began to tug at Morgan's arm. 'Mr Jackson says the sailors are going to catch one, and we're going to eat it for dinner.'

Following Charley up onto the deck, they joined the other passengers marvelling at the seething school of sharks.

'They've been drawn by the fishing net we've been trawling behind us for the last hour, ' explained Mr Sapsford.

Looking to where the sailors were working, Morgan saw Mr Quigley approaching Mr Jackson to ask him something. Mr Jackson shook his head and ushered the old man away from the bustle around the ropes and nets.

'I never thought I'd say this,' Mrs McPhail said, 'but I do confess that fish soup again for dinner is not something I'm relishing.'

'Never mind, Mrs McPhail,' said Mr Dempster jokingly, 'you can have shark for a change — the tiger of the sea.'

'But I thought it was a fish,' Mrs McPhail began, and then realised she was being teased. 'Oh, Mr Dempster, you are such a card.' She joined in the general laughter.

Behind him, Morgan heard Gordon mutter, 'Playing his cards right, if you ask me.'

After the sailors had managed to net a shark and dispatch it on deck, the adult passengers fell to their differing pursuits. The children, however, were still stimulated after the excitement of the sharks, and the two servants responsible for their care were unable to curb their energy. The two youngest Owens children, a rambunctious five-year-old boy and a precocious two-year-old girl, began running about up and down the steps leading to the quarterdeck.

When they took to jumping in and out of the piles of rope coiled near the masts, the Berkeley twins joined the game. In a mirror of the relationship between their respective parents, the youngest Sapsford girls followed their lead. The servants' remonstrations were ineffectual. And the muttered curses of the sailors were just 'noise', as far as the children were concerned.

Morgan generally avoided having anything to do with the children, partly due to his bachelor ignorance of what might be done, but also influenced by his observation that most parents seemed to resent the intrusion of others, regardless of how poorly behaved their children were. He sought to catch the eye of Lady Wood, but she was involved in animated discussion with the older children.

He couldn't see Mrs Berkeley or Mrs Sapsford, or their husbands. Mr Owens was deep in conversation with Mr Veitch, oblivious of the children. If the parents saw fit to ignore their children's behaviour then he decided it was none of his business. He turned his attention back to Gordon and Mr Dempster, who were busy arguing about the most likely date of their first sighting land.

There came a sudden piercing wail from one of the Berkeley twins who had tumbled down the steps.

The sound brought Mr Berkeley striding up on deck and Mr Sapsford racing behind out of breath. Mr Berkeley grabbed the child's arm roughly to put him back on his feet.

The other children who initially had run back down to the main deck to see what had happened to their friend, froze where they stood, too young yet to dissemble—they guiltily awaited their punishment as inevitable.

Morgan couldn't hear what Mr Berkeley hissed at his servant, but he could see her tired old face close off. She rapidly collected up the boy and the other younger children to take them down below. What he did hear was the outrage in Mr Berkeley's voice as he strode up to Mr Owens.

'What did you think you were doing, allowing your ragamuffins to run riot? I've told you before, Owens, I won't be letting my children play with them if they can't be controlled. They'll be seeing the back of my hand if this keeps up.'

Out of the corner of his eye, Morgan saw that Lady Wood was ushering the older Berkeley children away from the adults, leading Charley and Adelaide up to the quarterdeck and pointing to something out to sea. Mr Dempster took her lead and offered an arm each to Miss McPhail and her mother and moved in the same direction.

Mr Owens' face coloured, and he drew himself up to his full height. He was a well-built man whose muscled arms and thick neck sat uncomfortably with his gentleman's clothes, cheap as they were. 'Don't you even think of it, Berkeley. You'll have me to deal with if you so much as raise a hand to them.'

Gordon, who had been lounging in a chair by the rail, eyes closed in the sunshine, rose with surprising swiftness. Moving between the two angry men, he put a hand on Mr Owens' chest. 'No need for this, no need at all,' he said to each of them. 'Settle down and no harm's done.'

'Well, I'll be telling the captain that you threatened my children, Berkeley,' said Mr Owens.

Behind Mr Berkeley came Mr Sapsford's caution. 'And I'll be telling the captain that you threatened Mr Berkeley.'

'Jellyfish, Papa, come and look.' It was Adelaide's high voice carrying down to them.

Distracted, Mr Berkeley flicked himself in her direction, and the tension of the men's locked gaze broke. Mr Owens, still glaring belligerently, strode off. Mr Berkeley headed towards the quarterdeck. Mr Sapsford stood for a moment, irresolute. He went away, muttering under his breath, 'Well, the captain should know.'

Morgan and Gordon exchanged a glance.

Gordon then resumed his chair, closed his eyes again and said, 'I cannot imagine the captain's going to be none too keen on being woken, do you?'

The passengers clustered by the quarterdeck rail looked down to the ocean below at the jellyfish. Morgan saw wave upon wave crested with bright purple and blue translucent bubbles trailing long tangled tendrils. There was a whole colony of them. The rough margins, easily a hundred yards across, moved restlessly with the sea. James, their former assistant steward, was loitering nearby, clearly not engaged in his new duties among the sailors.

At Lady Wood's urging, Mr Jackson ordered him to throw over a bucket on a line to scoop up a few of them. As the bucket was hoisted up the side of the ship, they could see the long tentacles hanging below for five yards or more. Morgan, along with the other passengers, had seen them before—the sight not uncommon, as they washed up on the beaches around Sydney after big storms—but never this many.

'They're so big,' exclaimed Miss McPhail.

'Perhaps it's because we're seeing them out to sea,' Mr Dempster suggested. 'They always seem deflated by the time they wash up on shore in New South Wales.'

'The disappointment of their arrival, no doubt,' said Lady Wood. Turning to Charley and Adelaide, she added, 'I understand their scientific name is *Nauticulum*.'

Morgan winced internally as she said the wrong name. He would have corrected her, but he held back from doing so publicly. Their recent rapprochement was too fragile to endanger.

The children's faces were alight as she pointed out the different parts of the creature in the bucket at their feet, warning them of the severity of the sting from its tentacles.

'Can we take it down to show the others?' asked Adelaide.

'Can you lift the bucket, Charley?' Mr Berkeley asked.

Charley proudly lifted the bucket, and Morgan watched with some trepidation as he and Adelaide made their way slowly down the steps, water sloshing with each tread.

At Mr Berkeley's worried look, Mr Jackson said crossly, 'Go with them, James, and mind they don't get into any trouble.'

Mr Quigley waited at the base of the steps for the children to pass by, before asking, 'Mr Jackson, might I have a word?'

As promised, there was shark on the table at dinner, simply steamed, next to a jug of some indeterminate white sauce. Most of the other passengers stayed with the more familiar dishes, but Gordon helped himself with avidity.

'I think I may try some.' Lady Wood gestured to the dish, and Mr Quigley moved it within her reach.

Mrs Sapsford watched her closely. 'I may follow suit,' she said with an air of bravado. She served herself only a small portion, and she didn't go back for a repeated helping.

Between Gordon and Mr Veitch, the dish was nearly finished before Morgan managed to try a piece. The chunks of flesh were easy to disengage from the bones.

Mr Akers arrived late. 'No shark left?' he asked the steward, who nodded haughtily and took the dish away to replenish it.

'Your fault if you miss out because you're rude enough to be late to dinner,' grumbled the captain.

'My apologies. A call on my professional services. One of the Berkeley twins seems to have taken it upon himself to see if it is possible to detach a jellyfish's tentacles from its body. Nasty sting.'

'Oh, poor little mite,' said Mrs McPhail. 'Not the poor thing that fell down the steps earlier today, I hope?'

'Couldn't tell. I can't tell them apart,' he replied with his mouth half full. He swallowed and went on. 'Mind you, now it'll be easy. Huge red welts wrapped around both hands. He won't be touching much of anything for a while.'

Morgan realised neither Mr nor Mrs Berkeley were at dinner and experienced a rush of gratitude for his bachelor childfree state. Lady Wood was looking at him with an amused expression and, not for the first time, he felt she could read his mind.

As the others talked on, Lady Wood arose and left. Morgan assumed she was asking after the Berkeleys.

As she settled herself back beside him, she answered his unspoken question. 'I managed to catch James before he tossed the bucket of jellyfish over the side. I want to have another look at the jellyfish after dinner.'

'Is there something in particular you want to examine?'

'No, it's more that I keep worrying if I told the children the correct name. I thought if I drew a sketch then I could confirm it on some other occasion.'

Morgan smiled, pleased at having the opportunity to advise her. 'I think you'll find it's a Portuguese Man-of-War. Mr Akers has a copy of Alexander von Humboldt's work on such fauna. I can write down the Linnean classification for you, Lady Wood.'

Mr Akers nodded. 'It's wonderful to find a woman so interested in these matters, Lady Wood. Very happy to be of any assistance.'

Struck by Mr Akers' diplomacy, Morgan felt yet again the force of his lack of grace. He consoled himself with the thought that Lady Wood had twice asked for his advice. 'What did you think of the shark, Lady Wood?' he asked.

'I confess I am not sure the taste was much different from any other fish. However, our good ship's cook does seem to favour the same sauce for all his fish dishes.'

Mrs McPhail leaned across to say, 'Very heavy handed on the anchovy and horseradish, in my opinion.'

The captain was not interested in culinary matters. 'The child will have learnt a good lesson about dealing with wildlife. You've got to have respect for them to learn how to manage a wild animal. Take my native cats, for example.'

Morgan's heart pounded, and he couldn't prevent his gaze from slipping to Mr Jackson, who was sitting staring into his cup fixedly.

The captain went on. 'I can let them out and be sure of them returning as soon as I put some food for them in their cage.'

'In the meantime, one of the damn things has been ransacking my cabin, hunting for whatever tit-bits it can find,' snapped Gordon, his face reddened by wine and irritation.

'I swear there was one in my cabin last night,' said Mr Dempster.

Miss McPhail covered her mouth in horror. 'You didn't go near it, did you? They have a bite, which can fester—I've heard a bitten limb can swell up and the person can even die of it.'

'Managed to chase it out of my cabin,' Mr Dempster said with some pride.

The captain seemed to be getting angrier as he listened, trying to get a word in. 'It's as I said: you have to know how to tame them.'

'With all due respect, Captain, they're not like English cats.' Mr Jackson's tone was anything but respectful. 'Native cats seem quiet, but that doesn't mean they are any less wild. They'll go their own way regardless of how quiet they look on the outside.'

'Well, if I catch one in my cabin or anywhere near my birds again, then I'll not spare its life.' Gordon spoke with asperity, and Mr Dempster nodded his agreement.

Mr Quigley opened his mouth to speak.

Mr Jackson cut him off. 'They're worth a pretty penny when we get home, so I'm sure the captain will be keeping them close to hand.'

The captain, clearly discomfited, cleared his throat. 'Well, time for me to be getting on with the job. We've still got a lot of lost time to catch up on, what with how long we were becalmed. I'll leave you good people to your leisure.'

Reluctantly, Morgan agreed to be Mr Dempster's partner at loo. He would rather have partnered Gordon who, although he was in his cups, generally didn't argue about his debts, ever-mounting as they were. However, Miss McPhail had asked Gordon. The thought crossed Morgan's mind that perhaps Miss McPhail was not so blindly in love as to risk financial disadvantage.

They played for a while, focused on the game.

Morgan threw down an Ace of Hearts. 'That's an Ace of Hearts, Gordon,' he said to remind him Hearts were trumps.

Gordon put down a Nine of Spades. When it came to Morgan's turn again, he put down his last Heart, a Six.

Gordon put down a King of Hearts.

'What?' said Mr Dempster. 'You've made a revoke; you should have played that in your last turn.'

'No need to get upset,' Gordon said, slurring his words slightly. 'You did the same yourself not so long ago.'

'Yes, and I was fined five shillings for my oversight. We all agreed that was the penalty.' Mr Dempster looked over to where Mr Akers sat reading.

Mr Akers nodded vaguely as verification.

Morgan didn't recall Mr Dempster paying the fine; however, he trusted it was still recorded in their ongoing tally of their respective debts.

Miss McPhail's eyes were darting nervously from one to the other.

For a moment, Gordon's mouth opened to argue the point but, clearly too drunk to recall his last turn with any clarity, he simply shrugged and tossed in his cards. Miss McPhail put hers down in a neat pile, and Mr Dempster got up to help himself to another drink.

Morgan gathered the cards and shuffled them idly—more for something to do than with any intention of resuming the game.

Lady Wood left her conversation with Mr Akers nearby and came to sit opposite.

'Écarté, perhaps, Mr Mayhew?' she asked.

They had barely begun to play when the steward entered and bent over to talk quietly in Mr Akers' ear. 'That fool James has left the bucket full of jellyfish by the steps, and it's tipped across the deck. Now there's a bunch of sailors with stung feet. Mr Jackson says the night watch will be short if they can't be fixed up.'

Morgan saw Lady Wood fighting to suppress a smile. She put down her cards and said, affecting a yawn, 'I find I'm too fatigued for cards, after all, Mr Mayhew. I hope you will excuse me.'

He stood as she left but—rather than resume his seat—on impulse he decided to pursue her. 'Lady Wood,' he called, his voice coming out louder than he expected.

She turned, frowning slightly.

'I thought I should, must, say something.'

She waited for him to continue.

'Surely, you must say something to exonerate James.' His voice died away.

Lady Wood's face had frozen. 'I do not see I need to be explaining my actions to a young man such as yourself, Mr Mayhew. However, I will say this. These unfortunate consequences are entirely due to the location of the bucket. I'm sure you will agree, the location of it was entirely James' responsibility.'

He was transfixed by her icy beauty and struck through the heart by her tone.

She went on. 'I apologise if I have, by any inadvertent action, given rise to the impression you might think it proper to advise me on my actions.'

'No, no, not at all, Lady Wood,' he stammered. 'I only meant, I mean, it was not that, please, forget I spoke out of turn.'

There was a pause, and he found he couldn't meet her eye. He stared instead through the doorway where the twilight illuminated the deck. He heard her soft laugh and, in his shock, he looked back to find her smiling. He felt the light pressure of her gloved hand clasping his, only for a moment, and then gone.

'Ah, but we all forget ourselves from time to time, do we not? As do I, no doubt more often than I should,' she said, before turning and continuing towards her cabin.

Morgan gasped, suddenly remembered to breath and, seeking fresh air, walked out into the balmy late afternoon.

He paced up and down, trying to walk slowly to steady his heart rate. He was dimly aware of the limping shadows of the sailors passing to and from Mr

Akers' cabin. Over by the rail, he saw James on his knees with a pail and brush as he scrubbed the deck free of venom.

Chapter 16

A residue of the things unsaid

Henrietta

Henrietta couldn't face waiting in her cabin. The first watch would end at midnight, and Mr Jackson wouldn't be on until the next one. There was nothing she could do until then.

After her brief conversation with Mr Mayhew, she'd checked she knew where the bucket had been stowed and was confident that the number of sailors on deck would be fewer than usual. She'd already wrapped in oilskin both sets of documents within the one packet; all she had to do now was get it in the bucket for the handover.

Between Mr Nash and Mr Jackson, she'd managed to ascertain that the night would bring them nearer to the French coast than at any other time. However, their planned course would take them further west than the rendezvous point. Somehow, she had to convince Mr Jackson of the need to steer further east.

So far, her plan involved four bottles of her Uncle Herbert's claret, which she'd packed as gifts for her relatives. For the rest, she would have to extemporise.

Not wishing to draw attention to herself, by remaining on deck, she returned to the cuddy.

'Lady Wood, so lovely to have you back,' said Mrs McPhail. 'The gentlemen have been discussing whether to camp out again in the cuddy to escape the heat.'

Lieutenant Gordon said, 'Join me on deck. That's the place to be on a warm evening like this.'

Henrietta tried not to show her shock. *Has he divined my plans? But how could he?*

'I thought you stayed there so as to be nearer the grog,' said Mr Dempster.

Lieutenant Gordon's face flushed.

'At least we have the wind again; it is a little cooler,' Henrietta said.

'And hopefully we'll make better time,' said Mr Dempster. We don't want to run out of stores before landfall. The food has been getting atrocious.'

Henrietta joined Mr Mayhew in a game of whist against Mrs McPhail and Lieutenant Gordon. Miss McPhail sat nearby reading. Perhaps she had drawn enough likenesses of Mr Dempster, as he sat next to her, ostensibly reading too. He was paying more attention to the company than the words before him. Mrs McPhail liked to talk during the game, much to Lieutenant Gordon's annoyance, but Henrietta was happy to be distracted from what lay ahead.

'And we also had some dancing.' Mrs McPhail was catching Henrietta up on some of the activities she missed while confined to her cabin some days before. 'Mr Dempster and Bridget, and Mr and Mrs Berkeley, and Mr and Mrs Sapsford went through a set of reels while Mr Akers played his fiddle.

'And quite the scandal there was afterwards,' said Mr Dempster. He made a show of checking they couldn't be overhead. 'Perhaps inspired by their proximity and the heat of the moment, Mr Sapsford said, "Mrs Berkeley, may I have the pleasure of dancing with you".'

Mrs McPhail clicked her tongue. 'But they often talk. No scandal in that.'

Mr Mayhew had his hand to his mouth, suppressing his laughter.

Mr Dempster went on, with another exaggerated look over his shoulder. 'But then, Mr Berkeley went over to Mrs Sapsford and said "Mrs Sapsford, may I have the pleasure of dancing with you".'

Lieutenant Gordon sighed impatiently, waiting for Mrs McPhail to play her card. 'If a reel is so inspiring, imagine what a waltz might do.'

'Oh, we're quite modern, I assure you,' said Mrs McPhail. 'Waltzing is not at all uncommon these days. You can back me up, can't you, Lady Wood?'

Henrietta tried to keep her smile at bay and examined her cards closely.

Thankfully, Mr Mayhew made another effort to steer the topic into safer waters. 'Well, we can't blame dancing, with all its perils, for every scandal in the world. Scandals happen all the time, even among royalty,' he said.

'Especially among royalty,' said Henrietta. 'Think of Queen Caroline's trial.'

'They're too young to remember.' Mrs McPhail chuckled. 'What a to-do—the poor Queen.'

'We do all know about it, though,' said Miss McPhail. 'The King was trying to find an excuse to divorce her, wasn't he? I mean, she couldn't have had all those, those—' She broke off as she searched for a word that wouldn't embarrass her.

'The problem was mainly that Italian chappie, wasn't it? What was his name?' asked Mr Dempster.

'Permagui,' answered Henrietta. She had been in India at the time, and the gossip had been rife. However, she learnt more later from Sir Giles, because he had followed the events with great interest, as his patron, Lord Carter, was the Queen's advocate. The authority with which she spoke drew her listeners' gaze, and she went on. 'Did you know our very own Police Superintendent, Captain Rossi, was called as a witness?'

'No!' Mrs McPhail exclaimed.

The others were agreeably startled.

'What was it, that all the witnesses kept saying?' Lieutenant Gordon asked. 'Some Italian phrase.'

'*Non mi recordo,*' answered Henrietta. 'It means, "I don't recall".'

'Convenient,' said Mr Dempster. 'I'll remember that phrase for emergencies.'

'If you're going to do something scandalous, Mr Dempster,' said Henrietta, 'then you should treasure the memory, not lose it. Life is too short, don't you agree, to waste a single memory?'

Mr Mayhew said, 'I'm sure you've never done anything scandalous, Lady Wood.'

His gallantry irked her. It was extremely annoying the way young people made so many assumptions, as if age conferred dull respectability. *If only he knew what I planned to do, he'd soon change his mind.* Perhaps she should bring him into her confidence. But, no, whatever she was going to do tonight, she didn't want a witness.

Lieutenant Gordon gave up shuffling the cards. He was losing heavily and seemed to have given up hope of anyone concentrating on the game. 'You have some tales to tell, Lady Wood, which ones can you share?'

'Let me see.' She made a play of thinking back, shaking her head as if some thought was too scandalous to tell. 'Well, there was the time I dressed up as a man.'

'Oh,' exclaimed Miss McPhail. She so clearly clung to the affectations of a girl while each passing year etched the reality of her spinsterhood on her face. The girl—no, the woman—needed to grow up, whether or not she ever married.

'You didn't,' Mrs McPhail said, giggling.

Mr Mayhew stared at Henrietta in disbelief.

Henrietta shrugged. 'I thought Arthur might have told you this one, Mr Mayhew. It was while I was living at Aylesford. My brother Griffith was home on leave from his naval duties, and my brothers and sisters and I were making a historical tableau vivant in the parlour to depict the victory over Napoleon. Griffith was courting Mary Wood at the time, and so he was not with us, so I was able to use his dress uniform without his knowledge.'

'You've convinced me,' said Lieutenant Gordon, looking at her appraisingly.

'I'm sure you cut a fine figure,' said Mr Dempster.

Miss McPhail glared at him.

Mr Mayhew's face had not recovered from his shock, and she couldn't resist teasing him further. 'So, Mr Mayhew. What do you say?'

'I'm sure in the privacy of the family it must have,' he stammered, 'greatly enhanced the tableau. And of course, you were not a maid at the time, and such actions are perhaps less, less ...' He ran out of words. His gaze quailed when he looked into her laughing face and then fell to her lap, skittering away as if his eyes could touch her.

'Less dangerous?' she said, finishing his sentence. 'Yes, no doubt. Widows are strangely placed, are they not? In some ways they have freedoms that old maids do not, but in other ways their lives are more restricted in the things they do and in the company they keep.'

'There's no need for old maids or widows to go without company in a place like Sydney,' said Lieutenant Gordon. 'I've never been in a place with more men and so few women.'

'How many old maids are there, do you think,' asked Henrietta. She held up her fingers and began to count. 'Miss Jacob, um—'

'Never mind, Gordon, if Mrs Chisholm has her way there'll soon be more than enough young women for you in the Female Immigrants' Home,' said Mr Dempster, cutting in. He rose to his feet while Miss McPhail and her mother made their excuses and left. After an irresolute pause, he followed them.

Henrietta considered following suit. Sleep would be impossible in her current frame of mind, so she accepted Mr Mayhew's offer of another glass of wine instead.

'What were you saying before, about restrictions, Lady Wood?' Mr Mayhew asked, drawing his chair closer. 'From what Arthur and you have told me, I had formed the impression your life had been relatively free from restriction.'

'Strange isn't it, what each of us calls "restriction"? For me, the time in my father's house was prison. As a child, learning to curb my enthusiasm, learning my manners, learning to listen and not to be heard—it was freedom to sail to Calcutta. Living with the family again after the luxuries and indulgences of India—it was like being shackled all over again.' Her hands clenched with the anger of the memory. 'Oh, I tried. I tried so hard. I helped my mother with my younger brothers and sisters. I tried to keep my own children in check. But I had brought them up to breath freely, and yet under my father's roof, it fell to me to be the one who suffocated them.'

Now she had started, she found she couldn't stop. 'My father never hesitated to tell me how spoiled I was, how much a drain I was on his resources, and how every sign of liveliness in some way detracted from his precious respectability as a member of the Legislative Council. You know what they used to call him, don't you: the Protector of the Public Purse. He protected his own purse just as well. He effectively disinherited Griffith—there was nothing for him after he died. Father wouldn't so much as lend me the money for my trousseau.' It had been a long tirade, and she glanced about, embarrassed. To her relief, she found that, apart from Mr Quigley, who had fallen asleep in the corner of the sofa, she and Mr Mayhew were alone.

'So what sort of man was Sir Giles?' Mr Mayhew asked. 'If you don't mind me asking.'

'He was, he was—' The memory of his funny stories and his quiet, perceptive enjoyment of his family—it all swept over her. 'You know, he was once nearly arrested?'

'No,' said Mr Mayhew in shock.

'We were staying out at Aylesford one night after a family dinner, and Sir Giles voiced an opinion on some Burbridge financial matters. My father held strong views and considered Sir Giles' advice to be interference. He went on about it at some length. It was the sort of speech that might be reasonable for a father-in-law to give in some circumstances, but not to a fifty-year-old son-in-law who is the Chief Justice. Sir Giles held his temper, but after we had retired for the night he couldn't sleep—pacing the floor and vowing he wouldn't be staying under father's roof again. Eventually, I fell asleep and awoke to find him gone. He'd left a note to say he had headed off at first light to walk back into Sydney.'

'That's twenty miles,' objected Mr Mayhew.

'Yes indeed—he hated to ride. Even if we convinced him to take a horse, he would just lead it along. Well, when he came to the turnpike, the soldiers bailed him up, asking him who he was and his business. They didn't believe him, and so they threatened to lock him up.' She laughed. 'In the end, he convinced them to take him into Sydney, where he was identified, of course. Sir Giles thought it was an amusing story and often dined out on it—though, of course, without saying what had led to his adventure.'

'He always struck me as a true gentleman,' said Mr Mayhew. 'And he sounds like he was a good husband to you.' He paused and then added, 'It puts me in mind of the story you told me about the elephant. In a way, when you married him, you changed your mahout.'

Henrietta paused for a moment, taking in the implications of his comment. 'I hope, Mr Mayhew, you are not comparing me to an elephant.'

Later, back in her cabin, she dismissed Hill and lay down fully dressed on the bunk.

All those reminiscences; it was the old who talked so much about the past, while their juniors must wait patiently and then sigh discretely with relief when the stories of days gone by are over. Each time she talked with Mr Mayhew, she felt she had said too much. It made her feel old, the way he listened with that attentive look, rather than as someone to disagree with, to provoke, to tease, and certainly not to flirt.

But then again, his last comment had shown unexpected shrewdness.

The memory of borrowing money from Dr Foster for her trousseau still rankled all these years later. Mr Mayhew was right, of course. Marrying again had solved so many difficulties, and Sir Giles had been so generous, although he had so little apart from his salary.

She closed her eyes. All the stories about the past left a residue of the things unsaid, the things that would spoil the tale but were the things that mattered—the flotsam still caught in the tide of her thoughts.

Chapter 17

I fell in love

Henrietta

'Mr Jackson? Might I have a word?' Henrietta spoke quietly as she approached the first mate, wary of the looks of the few sailors who were about.

'Lady Wood? Bit late for you, isn't it?'

The full moon reflected off the water, casting Mr Jackson's rough features into hard relief.

'I confess I have been unable to sleep.' She held out the bottles of wine. 'I thought I might have a drink to help me sleep, but I'd prefer not to drink alone.' She took a deep breath. 'And, I owed you an apology. You know, about your men being stung.'

Mr Jackson only took a moment to decide. He reached out for the bottles. 'Well, that's a mighty fine gesture, milady. I don't mind telling you the captain was none too pleased. Told me it was all my fault. I thought for a while there I might be joining James scrubbing the deck.' Mr Jackson wrestled the corks out of the bottles with his knife and handed one back to her. After taking a deep draught from his own, he said, 'Well, I have to say, this here drop is taking the sting out.'

Henrietta joined him in laughing at his joke. It didn't take long for the usually taciturn Mr Jackson to become loquacious. She restricted herself to small sips from her bottle, as she was inducted into the dull story of Mr Jackson's much-imposed-upon life. He proved to be the sort of man who was silent only because no one had ever thought him interesting enough to ask him a question. Talking didn't stop him from drinking, and Henrietta decided she'd better introduce her request quickly or face sacrificing her own bottle and the two she had held in reserve.

'You have had such a hard life, Mr Jackson, and seen much of the world,' she said, casting about for inspiration. 'I feel like I could confide in you. I could trust you to help me if I were in need, couldn't I? Even if it were a little irregular, shall we say?'

Mr Jackson's eyes narrowed. 'How irregular?'

'Oh, nothing illegal, Mr Jackson, I assure you. It's just that a long time ago when I was hardly more than a girl …' Henrietta waited for him to exclaim it couldn't have been very long ago, but Mr Jackson was not a man of breeding. She went on. 'I'm afraid I fell in love with a—with a Frenchman.'

Mr Jackson took a long pull at the bottle. 'Well, that's not exactly treason, now is it?'

'No, but you see, we exchanged letters.' She sighed. 'And you know what young love is.'

'Aye, I do that,' Mr Jackson said, looking flattered to have the assumption made about him.

'Well, I wrote some things I would not wish anyone else to read. And, as it transpired, just as I kept and treasured his letters, so the Frenchman kept mine. But, you see, he has passed on.' Henrietta gave a sob, so completely caught up in her story she could have been watching de Bougainville's ships sail out of the harbour. 'And his relatives have found my letters.'

'Blackmail?'

'Of a sort,' she said. 'They promise to destroy them, but only if I hand over his letters to them.'

'But what do you think I can do? Do you need them delivered when we get to London? That'd be no trouble, milady.'

Henrietta was pleased to note that Mr Jackson needed to concentrate more than usual on enunciating his words. But, she needed to move him along if he wasn't to become too drunk to assist her. 'You see it all so clearly, Mr Jackson. Yes, I do need your help to deliver them. But, with the troubles brewing in France, they insist I deliver the letters directly to their hands.'

'What? They want you to go to France? That's not safe these days. Particularly for the gentry, like. Meaning no offence, ma'am, milady.'

'No, they are sending one of their ships to rendezvous with us. I have the coordinates,' she said, trying to stem any objections. 'It's only a few miles out of our way.'

Mr Jackson took the slip of paper over to the ship's lantern and examined it.

Henrietta moved closer. *What else will it take for me to do this?*

Mr Jackson wasn't so drunk he couldn't strike a bargain. 'Would you be having any more of this fine wine, then, milady?'

Relieved, Henrietta retrieved the other two bottles. 'One when we change course, and one after we've dropped the letters.'

Once the ship was set on its new course, so that the bucket with the documents could be lowered down and passed to them, Henrietta permitted herself a deep draught from the bottle she clutched in her hand. Her other hand guarded the packet of documents tucked firmly to her waist by her shawl; she needed to find an opportune moment to put the documents in the bucket.

She leaned against the rail, peering across the moon-washed ocean. She was grateful Mr Jackson was keeping his distance. He'd bought the cooperation of the midshipman by sharing the bottles she'd handed over, and Henrietta caught snatches of their singing.

Her head was beginning to droop when she suddenly became aware of a brilliant brightness around her. The waves rippling from the ship began to take on a luminous glow, breaking and reforming as they disturbed the surface of the water.

'Pretty, isn't it?'

Henrietta turned, expecting to find Jackson. It was Lieutenant Gordon.

'Phosphorescence,' Lieutenant Gordon said. 'Some type of plankton, they say.'

Henrietta couldn't reply. The night air was still warm, but she was as cold as if the ship was passing an iceberg.

'I think your wait might be over,' he said, nodding to a dark shape breaking its way through the glittering sea. 'Are you sure you can manage that bucket by yourself?'

Is he offering to help me? She couldn't take it in. Or would he grab the documents as soon as she pulled the packet out? 'Yes,' she said stiffly, only her eyes travelling to where the bucket was stowed, mere feet away.

Lieutenant Gordon eyed her shrewdly. 'Maybe on a good day, Lady Wood, but not with that hand of yours.'

Henrietta was about to protest, when out from the shadows another figure emerged.

Mr Mayhew.

She looked first to one and then to the other, but no explanation was forthcoming.

There was a burst of laughter from the sailors. Evidently, more of them had deserted their posts, lured by the prospect of drink.

Mr Mayhew glanced nervously in their direction.

'How many bottles did you give them?' Lieutenant Gordon asked him.

'Four,' Mr Mayhew replied.

'That's not going to last much longer. Leave it with me.' Lieutenant Gordon began to head towards the singing. 'When they come along side, Mayhew, they'll lose the wind, so you've only got seconds for them to get hold of the bucket. Best lower it in readiness.'

Henrietta began to shake, every nerve in her body alive. With Mr Mayhew's appearance, her fears about Lieutenant Gordon melted away. Griffith had been wrong about him. Lieutenant Gordon could easily have left her to her own devices. Without his instructions, she would have waited until it was too late.

She picked up the bucket, but Mr Mayhew moved to assist. It was heavy, the oak wood wet and held fast by iron rings. The rope secured to the handle was sodden and rough. Lieutenant Gordon had been right about that too. She didn't have the strength to lower the bucket with her burned hand.

In silhouetted shadows, Lieutenant Gordon was passing his whiskey flask around the gathered sailors. None of them were going to notice what she and Mr Mayhew were doing.

'It'll be on us any minute,' whispered Mr Mayhew.

Looking back to the ocean, the approaching ship was closing in fast.

She delved into her shawl, fighting to retrieve the packet.

She thrust it into the base of the bucket, pushing it down so it lay securely.

Mr Mayhew hoisted the bucket to the rail.

The approaching ship was no more than a sloop really, much smaller than the *Lord Henderson*, and bearing full sail in its efforts to pace them, if only for the seconds the transfer would require.

Mr Mayhew let the bucket down over the side and began to release the rope, the bucket swinging wildly from side to side in the swell. But he was losing his grip and the only thing she could do was grab hold of it with him to try to brake the speed of the bucket's descent. The coarse rope seared across the palms of her hands. She was almost grateful for the burns from the lamp — at least one of her hands had the protection of being wrapped in a gauze bandage.

Mr Mayhew's knuckles were bone white in the moonlight as he clenched his hands tightly around the rope. She bent over the railing, her arms stretched out, trying to steady the swing of the bucket.

The sloop sailed underneath the dangling bucket.

'Now,' Mr Mayhew whispered hoarsely.

They let go.

Chest heaving, she peered down, trying to see where the bucket had landed.

Horrified, she saw it clip the sloop's deck and teeter over. If it fell, it would be crushed between the sloop and the side of the *Lord Henderson*.

But then, with no wind in its sails, the sloop seemed to move back out of view, as the *Lord Henderson* ploughed ahead.

'No!' Mr Mayhew shrieked, as Henrietta whirled away and began to run.

She raced up to the poop deck, oblivious to the drinking sailors. On the sloop, she made out against the softly waning glow of the phosphorescence the shape of a man standing at the bow of the sloop, holding a bucket triumphantly aloft.

Her heart soared at the sight. But then Henrietta's elation choked in her throat. The eyes of sailors were upon her.

'How about a bit more of this whiskey, if any of you good fellows have a mind?' said Lieutenant Gordon, drawing attention away from her.

She shrank back into the gloom. The darkness was giving way to the deep blue pre-dawn. On deck, there were more sailors than before. The next watch was starting.

She couldn't stay on deck. The sooner she returned to her cabin, the less noticeable she'd be.

Making her way back through the dim hatchway, she was caught off guard by a movement behind her.

With a jarring thud, her back was pressed against the wall.

'I think you owe me a favour, Lady Wood,' growled a man's voice. Mr Jackson pushed his large bulk into her. His chest was level with her eyes.

She couldn't breathe.

She wriggled, desperately trying to manoeuvre past him.

'That's a treat,' he said, the weight of his full body against her. 'You can keep that up.'

'Let me get past. I shall call for the captain.' Henrietta tried to sound authoritative.

Mr Jackson bent his head to hers. 'Now, I'm thinking you don't want to be bothering the captain with what you've been up to tonight, milady.'

She was engulfed by the stink of his hot breath. His whiskers scraped along her cheek. The more she tried to free herself, the closer he pressed, rubbing himself against her. She swallowed hard.

'Enough,' Mr Mayhew roared, stepping forward.

Mr Jackson drew back a fraction.

The momentary release was enough. She slammed her knee into Mr Jackson and he collapsed in on himself, swinging down and away from her, emitting a strangled groan.

Mr Mayhew escorted her back to her cabin in silence.

She wanted to know how he'd come to be on deck at all, let alone with Lieutenant Gordon. Had he worked out her plan and, unwittingly, involved Lieutenant Gordon? Or had it been the other way around and the lieutenant had known about her mission all along? *But then, why did Griffith warn me about him?*

She paused after opening the cabin door, wanting to invite him inside, so she could find out. But by the time she'd turned around, he'd gone.

Chapter 18

Insinuations

Morgan

With little enthusiasm, Morgan viewed the selection of food laid out on the sideboard for breakfast, before settling himself beside Gordon.

They exchanged a nod, as if to acknowledge it had been a good night's work.

But had it been?

He was not entirely sure what the events of the previous night were about. All he knew was that Gordon, who'd not previously sought his company and who Lady Wood seemed to ignore, had woken him in the dead of night telling him that Lady Wood needed their assistance. Of course, he had complied.

'Never mind, Mr Mayhew,' said Mrs Berkeley. She was already seated and busily working her way through a large plate of devilled kidneys. 'Some of the salted pork is left.'

Mrs Sapsford said with a grumble, 'It's all very well the captain saying the stores are to be used up, but I can't understand why things haven't been better managed.'

'I quite agree, Mrs Sapsford,' said Mr Sapsford. 'We're passing up to twenty ships each day. Surely some arrangements might be made.'

Mrs Sapsford threw a quick glance over her shoulder and then said, conspiratorially to Mrs Berkeley, 'So do you think the rumour is true?'

Despite himself, Morgan looked up from his meal.

Mrs Berkeley nodded. 'I wouldn't be at all surprised.' Noticing Morgan's interest, she whispered, 'We think Mr Dempster might have proposed, but we don't know if Miss McPhail has accepted.'

Gordon stared with a sour eye at the sausage on Morgan's plate.

'I don't think there's any question, is there? A bird in the hand, and all that,' said Mrs Sapsford.

'About time too, if you ask me,' said Mr Quigley. 'The chap's been taking far too many liberties. The least he can do.'

Gordon got up abruptly and left.

At the sound of the McPhails approaching the cuddy, Mrs Sapsford put her finger to her lips. Mrs McPhail bustled over to the sideboard followed by Miss McPhail. Mrs McPhail looked extremely cheerful, but Miss McPhail kept her eyes averted, her head down.

Mr Dempster hung back a little, talking with Joseph McPhail before he caught sight of what was on the sideboard. 'We can't get there soon enough. And if we don't make up for the lost time, then this young man,' he said, gesturing to Joseph, 'will be skin and bone by the time we arrive.'

'Lost time? Why, the wind's been fair, hasn't it?' asked Mr Berkeley.

Mr Dempster settled himself at the table, grinning in anticipation of telling his news. 'Well, anyone who was out on deck this morning heard all about it. The captain and Mr Jackson were having a right set-to. The captain was yelling, "Why didn't you let me know when you found out?" And Mr Jackson was yelling back that there was nothing to be done but get the ship back on course. Mr Jackson had only just been promoted to first mate for this voyage, but the captain says he'll be reporting him to the owners when we get back to London. But Jackson says—' He paused for effect. 'Lady Wood's the one to blame.'

Morgan drank his tea with deliberation.

It was left to the other passengers' questions and exclamations to prompt Mr Dempster to explain further.

'Well,' Mr Dempster said, clearing trying not to laugh, 'apparently, Lady Wood kindly offered some of the sailors some wine last night—rather a lot of wine if we can judge by the consequences. When Mr Nash came to relieve Jackson from his watch at four this morning, he found the ship had gone off course. We could have ended up on the French coast, by the sound of the fuss the captain was making.'

The Berkeleys, Sapsfords and McPhails united in a medley of disapproval and astonishment. Mr Quigley sighed and resumed eating, shaking his head.

Under the cover of the hubbub, Mr Dempster said to Morgan quietly, 'We can hardly blame Jackson, can we? Lady Wood's charms would be most beguiling by moonlight, after all.'

Engulfed with conflicting emotions, Morgan rose and started to pick among the remnants of food still on the sideboard. *How dare Dempster make such insinuations?* He tried to put his confused thoughts of Lady Wood aside.

'And the worst of it is, we could have been home so much sooner,' Mr Dempster said in a louder voice, looking over at Miss McPhail, who blushed.

'Well, that helps make our decision as to when to leave the ship,' said Mr Berkeley, addressing Mrs Berkeley. 'I'll speak to the captain and ask if we can arrange for the pilot to take us off at Brighton. They've built a railway from Brighton to London—that would be a new experience for us all.'

Mrs Berkeley pursed her lips tightly. Morgan got the impression this was a conversation the Berkeleys had been having for a while. When Morgan thought about it, he couldn't imagine the difficulties in managing the early disembarkation of seven children.

'Yes, an excellent idea, Mr Berkeley,' said Mr Sapsford.

Mrs Sapsford and Mrs Berkeley exchanged a look.

'Perhaps we should do likewise?' Mrs McPhail put to Joseph and Miss McPhail.

'Yes, the quicker we land, the better,' said Joseph McPhail, but Miss McPhail didn't answer.

'A wonderful idea, Mrs McPhail,' said Mr Dempster. 'I discussed the exact same plan with Lieutenant Gordon, but he wouldn't join me. He's determined to stay on board all the way to St Katherine Docks, though I can't think why.'

Morgan reflected that Mr Dempster knew very well why Gordon would be avoiding the additional cost of taking a train to London. Gordon's losses at cards during the voyage were heavy, and after discharging what he still owed the captain, it would be surprising if there was much left. In fact, the same reasoning would apply to Mr Dempster, but if he travelled with the McPhails, perhaps he wouldn't be footing the bill.

'So do you think we have been much delayed?' asked Mrs Berkeley. 'I mean, if the ship does make up the time, when do you think we might reach Brighton? I'm thinking of the packing that needs to be organised in the time.'

'There was a stiff breeze when I was out on deck earlier,' said Mr Dempster. 'The captain tells me that we might catch the first sight of land by tonight.'

Mr Quigley said, 'If so, and if it's anything like my last trip, we could be passing Brighton the day after tomorrow.'

'So soon,' said Mrs McPhail, her brows furrowed. 'I haven't even started my packing either. I had thought to stay on board all the way to London.'

Miss McPhail gave a brief nod, almost involuntarily.

'I can see that is your preference, Miss McPhail,' Mr Dempster said. 'Although, as usual, you are avoiding putting your own wishes ahead of everyone else.'

'Well, that settles it,' Mrs McPhail said. 'We'll do as we planned originally, and stay on board.'

'An excellent decision, Mrs McPhail,' said Mr Dempster. 'I am quite swayed by your arguments and shall do the same.'

Morgan had no reason to check the cages of the few birds that had survived the journey—none were his, but he sought refuge below decks as he mulled over the implications of the previous night.

It had been a shock to see Lady Wood thrusting the packet into the bucket. It smelled of espionage. Had he been a patriot or had he committed treason? The former, he hoped.

Whatever the reason, Lady Wood's behaviour had been extraordinary.

Plying the sailors with drink? Probably with her uncle's finest claret, knowing her tastes.

The sailors' grog was watered down at the best of times and, as they were reaching the end of the voyage, the last remaining supply would be barely quarter strength. Her claret would have been as strong as whiskey to them. No wonder they'd be happy to oblige.

But it had brought her into such danger. If he hadn't followed her from the deck …

He was still churning when young Joseph McPhail joined him.

'You've still got three alive,' Morgan told him, trying to be pleasant.

Joseph glanced at them without interest. 'Mr Mayhew?'

Morgan turned to give him his full attention.

'I'm wanting to ask for your assistance, if I may.'

'Of course,' said Morgan, surprised. 'You might be better to ask an older gentleman, though, Mr Quigley perhaps or Mr Berkeley.'

'No, no,' said Joseph, 'I couldn't be asking them.'

Intrigued, Morgan waited for Joseph to go on.

'It's about Bridget,' he said, and then it all came rushing out. 'You see, since our father died, it's been my mother and my sister and myself, and there's a lot of worry. Well, my mother has a lot of worry. My father left us well provided for, and when my mother passes on, Bridget will have no one to look after her. I tell her I'll look after Bridget, but she says, once I've got myself a wife, I'll have other responsibilities. And so, she wants Bridget to be married so she'll be all right. But Bridget, well Bridget is getting a bit older and so the sort of men who have been paying their respects, well, they're not particularly well off themselves, if you get my meaning.'

'Mm.' Morgan didn't know what to say. Perhaps less said, the better.

'And, you know Mr Dempster has proposed?'

So the rumour was not baseless. Morgan had shared the other passengers' concerns about Mr Dempster's over-familiarity, but then, that was Mr Dempster's style—he meant nothing by it.

Joseph continued, 'And I was thinking, you are acquainted with Mr Dempster and might have formed an idea of his character, and you could—'

'Could give you my opinion?'

'No, no,' said Joseph hurriedly.

Morgan was at a loss.

'It's Lieutenant Gordon I'm worried about,' explained Joseph. 'Bridget has been crying and upset, ever since Mr Dempster proposed. It turns out she was hoping Lieutenant Gordon would be the one doing the asking. But Lieutenant Gordon—'

'Has no money and fewer prospects.' Morgan grasped the problem. 'But it sounds as though you don't need to be worrying, Joseph, if, as you say, Lieutenant Gordon has not declared himself.'

'But ...' Joseph's face coloured. 'Bridget is saying that perhaps the only reason he hasn't is that he thinks Mr Dempster has, if you get my drift. And so, she means to speak to Lieutenant Gordon about it, even though our mother has strictly forbidden her to do so.'

'Ah.'

Joseph soldiered on and said, 'I thought if someone, someone she respects, could have a word to her?'

'You're not suggesting that I—?' Morgan said, horrified at the thought of raising such a matter with Miss McPhail.

'No, no. I thought Lady Wood might—but I couldn't be asking her, but perhaps you could, on my behalf?'

Morgan's initial relief was dampened by evidence of the passengers' assumptions about the closeness of his and Lady Wood's friendship. 'I'm sorry, Joseph. I can see the situation is delicate. But give it some time, I'm sure things will work themselves out. You're a good brother to worry about your sister.' He patted Joseph's shoulder as he made his way back up toward the cabins.

Morgan flung himself down on the bed and relocated his place in *The Mysteries of London*. Distracted by the illustration of the young woman lying on her bed, he found it difficult to concentrate as he read:

It seemed as if some cunning hand had purposely arranged them all so as to strike the eye in a manner calculated to encourage the impression that this elegant boudoir was inhabited by a man of strange feminine tastes, or a woman of extraordinarily masculine ones.

Morgan had been staring at the same page without taking anything in for at least five minutes. And yet, he couldn't have said what he had been thinking about instead.

He tried again, reading aloud for a short while.

'A mass of luxuriant light chestnut hair, which flowed down upon her back, her shoulders, and her bosom; but not so as altogether to conceal the polished ivory whiteness of the plump fair flesh. The admirable slope of the shoulders, the swan-like neck, and the exquisite symmetry of the bust were descried even amid those masses of luxuriant and shining hair'.

He tossed the book on the bunk.

What he wanted to do was to shout at someone, about what he didn't know. Well, yes, he did know. When it came down to it, he didn't believe that Lady

Wood would have behaved as she had unless it was for some sound reason.

He paced two steps to the door and then back—the cabin so small that was all the movement it would allow.

After two more turns back and forth, he had it.

When he put together every extraordinary thing she had done on this voyage, it all started to make sense.

Lady Wood spent an inordinate amount of time with Mr Nash asking about navigation. She leapt from one end of the ship to the other at the sight of following ships. She charmed him into collecting a packet of documents in a most secretive manner. And lastly, she ventured on deck in the middle of the night and was responsible for the ship changing course.

He should have seen it before, but her constant supply of outrageous stories had somehow obscured the oddity of her actions. Whatever she had been doing, she had been planning it from the start of the voyage.

He needed to find out the truth.

Joseph McPhail's request gave him the perfect excuse for approaching her discreetly in her cabin.

He'd reached the top of the steps when he heard loud banging ahead.

Captain Gallagher was pounding on the door of Lady Wood's cabin. 'Lady Wood, I need to be having a word with you.'

The tone of his voice was so belligerent that Morgan stepped forward to intervene. Before he could do so, the door swung suddenly inward, catching the captain in motion as he struck the door. The captain staggered into the room, carried by his own momentum coinciding with the roll of the ship.

Running to the doorway, Morgan saw them, glaring, each waiting for the other to speak.

The captain broke first. 'Lady Wood, my apologies for disturbing you,' he said stiffly.

'Apology accepted. If you will, I prefer the privacy of my cabin.' She motioned towards the door, including Morgan in her gesture of icy dismissal.

Once on deck, Morgan headed to the poop deck. He gripped the rail, the sharp wind in his ears.

Below, on the main deck, he saw Mr Dempster deep in conversation with Miss McPhail. Mr Dempster's face bent close to hers, and from time to time he would grasp her hand. Morgan looked for Mrs McPhail but clearly she had decided to continue exercising her chaperoning duties with discretion. She and Mrs Berkeley were chatting, oblivious to children buzzing around them like bees.

In an effort to still his agitation, Morgan moved to join Mr Quigley and Mr Veitch, who were in the final stages of their morning's first game of chess. Morgan knew better than to break their concentration and so just nodded briefly as he sat nearby.

'Check,' said Mr Veitch, removing a piece from the board.

'And mate,' said Mr Quigley, sliding his Rook into position.

Mr Veitch repressed a sigh and set about arranging the pieces for a rematch. 'So we don't have the pleasure of Lady Wood's company this morning, Mr Mayhew?'

Morgan fought back his irritation. Why would the man think he was responsible for accounting for Lady Wood's movements? 'Evidently not,' he said.

Undeterred, Mr Veitch added, 'I should be surprised if she shows her face for the remainder of the voyage. Mrs Veitch speaks highly of her, but that's only because Lady Wood's the only one of the ladies who has thought fit to visit Mrs Veitch while she's been confined to her cabin. She hasn't been in a position to see how inappropriately Lady Wood has been in company. As I was telling Mrs Veitch the other day—'

Mr Quigley interrupted and said, 'Your move, if memory serves.'

Morgan left them to their game.

Joseph McPhail and young Charley Berkeley leaned over the rail of the quarterdeck. They were watching the sailors scraping the sides of the ship clean to prepare it for painting when they docked. The men balanced precariously on a plank hung from ropes slung over the side. Despite being tied around their waists, in the constant movement of the ship, the risks involved made the scene compelling. The boys stopped talking initially but started up again when Morgan leaned with them and looked down at the sailors.

Lady Wood didn't appear all day.

In the evening, Morgan found himself standing by the rail again. He had spent most of his time on deck, hoping for an opportunity to speak with her. No doubt she felt embarrassment and hoped to avoid any expression of ill will from the other passengers. He would, in her position. But then, thinking over her stories, he wondered if indeed his suppositions were correct. If embarrassment was the price for acting as you wished, it struck him that this was a currency Lady Wood had been comfortable trading all her life.

In the deepening twilight, he caught a short blink of light, well down on the horizon. He watched and waited. There it was again.

Mr Nash came to join him by the rail. 'That'll be the lighthouse from St Agnes—we've made good time today—234 miles. Nearly home, Mr Mayhew.'

Chapter 19

Departures and arrivals

Henrietta

By the following morning, Henrietta had recovered her composure enough to brave joining the other passengers on deck. She'd spent the previous day asleep, exhausted after the night's exertions. When not sleeping, she'd been content to lay back on her pillow, enjoying the memory of the night before. She wished she were a singer—this new story of hers was worthy of an opera. Oh, what a tale she'd make of it one day.

She sat quietly, keeping her hands—wounds freshly dressed—gloved and tucked in her muff, cradling them against having to move too much.

Her irritation with the other passengers—their voices, their bearing, even by the pores in their faces—rose with every hour, as if, through having been long repressed during the voyage, her sensitivities had been magnified. Henrietta doubted she would see any of them again after arrival, despite the sudden rush of each passenger to exchange their cartes de visite.

The Sapsfords handed around daguerreotype portrait cards. Henrietta couldn't see why people felt the need to provide a picture of themselves to others who were all too well acquainted with their countenance.

As she walked along the deck, Mr Mayhew fell into step. After the routine exchange of pleasantries, he remained silent. He hadn't spoken about their night on deck yet. Despite herself, she felt impelled to explain. They both spoke at once.

'Did you sleep—' started Mr Mayhew.

'Sleep has been—' she began.

'My apologies,' said Mr Mayhew. 'Do go on.'

'I feel I owe you an explanation, Mr Mayhew. You have been a real friend to me on this voyage. No, no, let me go on.'

It didn't take long to explain. As she'd half-expected, Mr Mayhew had already found his way to understanding her.

'But why would you put yourself in danger?' he asked.

'I confess my motives were not entirely altruistic. I extracted certain promises from the governor regarding support for my receiving a full pension. And not only for myself,' she hastened to add. 'Lady Ferris, as well.'

'Ah, so that's what Alfred kept insinuating. I should have guessed. But why didn't you keep hold of them? Now the documents are delivered directly to the French—'

'Oh.' Henrietta waved a gloved hand airily. Regretting the sudden painful motion, she eased her hand back into her muff. 'The governor's death put paid to that. Lord Grey has no reason to oblige. But, you know, I think now it wasn't really about the money at all. No,' she said with a laugh, 'don't be so sceptical. Riches come and go, but adventures—they're the stuff of memories. You're familiar with the Longfellow poem, I'm sure.'

Mr Mayhew stopped, waiting for her recitation.

'In the world's broad field of battle; In the bivouac of Life; Be not like dumb, driven cattle! Be a hero in the strife! Trust no Future, howe'er pleasant! Let the dead Past bury its dead! Act, act in the living Present! Heart within, and God o'erhead!'

They walked a little further.

'But then, you know that, don't you?' she said. 'Coming to my aid to collect the second packet, and again the other night, and yet again with what followed. You're a man who doesn't refuse adventure when it comes his way. Though I confess I haven't been able to work out how you even came to be there, at all. Did you call upon Lieutenant Gordon for support?'

'You give me too much credit, Lady Wood. It was Lieutenant Gordon who sought my aid. He seemed to know what was going on, though I couldn't say how.'

'Mm,' she said, putting the mystery away for the moment. 'You keep a journal, I think? So you can review your diary someday and fill in the missing pieces of your memory.'

He laughed. 'But, when I do look back at my journal, I find my whole life seems to have been a stream of trivial matters. Many of the important things that I recall are given scant mention, if at all.'

'If that is the case, it is no wonder I recall departures and arrivals so well. It is as if what happened in between did not exist.'

'I remember the shock of arriving in England from Jamaica,' said Mr Mayhew. 'The fog was so thick I could barely see my aunt down on the wharf, and my mouth was filled with the gritty taste of coal fires.'

Henrietta was following her own line of thought. 'I felt lost when my brother and I arrived in Calcutta. We had been taken off the budgerow at the *ghat* in darkness, and I had been much too excited to have slept. My uncle's house was haunted with servants all in white muslin—their dark faces disappearing in dim lamplight. They were ghosts, beckoning me on until we reached the dining hall. It was a palace to my eyes, though of course there were many finer in Calcutta, with rows of white, marble columns and a black and white tiled floor. Turbaned servants stood around the edges of the room, working the pulleys to move the huge fans suspended overhead.'

'You should write it all down. You should write about this voyage. I tell Lucy to write—she remembers her mother, Aunt Agnes, faced the negro uprising alone, totally dependent on the loyalty of their own blackies.'

At the mention of his aunt, Henrietta was struck, not for the first time, of the complexities involved in a marriage between first cousins. Unthinkingly, she chuckled. 'So, you are lucky in a sense to already know your future mother-in-law as a member of your family.'

'Not everyone would say the same,' Mr Mayhew replied eventually. 'When my sister and I returned to England, our care was partly in the hands of Sir Edward Doughty Tichborne. Please don't think me ungrateful,' he added hurriedly. 'Sir Edward has been a true friend and patron. He's the reason I have been able to purchase livestock and a share in the property.'

'But he does not approve of your marriage?' Henrietta asked.

'He's a Roman Catholic, and you know their views on the matter—and of course he didn't hesitate to share them with me. He didn't go so far as to withhold his financial support, but for a while I thought that might be the case.'

'Is that why you delayed so long in telling your aunt? I am sure you don't need to worry.'

They continued walking, and perhaps the personal nature of their conversation showed in their manner as, although many of their fellow passengers were on deck, no one approached.

Mr Mayhew blurted, 'I am so fortunate in being able to marry Lucy. She is exactly the sort of wife a man in my position should have—good company, my good friend, and a woman with experience of the realities of the colonial life. She will be the best kind of wife and mother to our children.'

Henrietta wondered if her husbands had considered their choice of a wife in such practical terms. Is that what Patrick considered when he proposed—a lively friend, the daughter of a gentleman, and an avenue to partnership in her uncle's company? Is that what Sir Giles thought—an engaging companion, a respectable widow, a stepmother for his growing children? So then, if the contract of marriage brought with it obligations and expectations, they had fulfilled theirs, and she had fulfilled her part.

She had indeed had a most fortunate life, she thought, unlike poor Mrs Veitch and all the women whose contract had been broken. It was then that she made her decision. It would hurt to hand over her winnings from cards, but that money could provide Mrs Veitch with escape, while she had only thought of a new hat to replace the one squashed in her hatbox.

On their last evening, there was no dessert with dinner—not so much as a biscuit—but there were no complaints from the passengers, so intent on the prospect of a proper meal once they arrived.

Fortunately, stores had not run so low as to diminish the supply of port after dinner, and so it was with considerable good humour they joined in a last game of cards. In the goodwill of parting, even Henrietta was invited to play. At one shilling a game, the pot grew quickly.

Lieutenant Gordon bowed out early, while Mr Dempster hung in a little longer. With a float from his father, Charley Berkeley was excited to join the adults for the game. His sister looked on enviously. She whispered instructions while peering over his hand, much to his chagrin and the ability of the other players to adjust their moves accordingly. Joseph McPhail and Mrs McPhail looked to be the winners for a while; however, Henrietta trumped Mrs McPhail, but then fell to Joseph.

'So, how have you fared?' Henrietta asked Mr Mayhew while the passengers clustered about Mr Akers, who was tallying up the daily record of wins, losses and promissory notes over the voyage.

'With this evening's nine-shilling win, for the voyage as a whole, I'm very nearly quits, despite my losses at loo,' Mr Mayhew replied.

Henrietta wondered how 'nearly quits' converted into currency but decided not to ask. She and Mr Mayhew had shared too much today.

The passengers began to settle their accounts with each other.

Mr Berkeley stood, looking over Mr Akers' shoulder. 'So, don't forget our wager—one hundred and two days for the voyage has lost you ten shillings, Mr Akers.'

Mr Akers' eyes narrowed as he shot a look at Henrietta and drew his money-purse out of his pocket.

Mr Dempster joined them, sitting down with a sigh. 'That was four pounds, which some would say could have been better spent, I suppose.' He glanced in Mrs McPhail's direction. 'Still,' he said, looking more cheerful, 'Gordon has lost more—six or seven pounds at least.'

Lieutenant Gordon poured himself a large drink before leaving.

Henrietta caught his eye and, at his nod, she rose to follow him.

Once out of earshot, he stopped and faced her. 'P'raps best you not be heading on deck now it's getting dark,' he said with a hint of a wink.

'I didn't want to miss the opportunity to thank you, Lieutenant Gordon, for your help. I confess myself surprised, however. My brother—'

'Your brother thinks that just because I support the Chartist cause, I'm not a patriot. But I had my orders from Governor Gipps, and his death or no, I did my best to carry them out.'

When Henrietta returned to the cuddy, it was to find the passengers still bemoaning their losses.

'There are no winners at cards after all. Poor Joseph is down by four pounds, but that will serve as a lesson to him.' Mrs McPhail kept her eye on Mr Dempster as she spoke.

'So, does anyone have any budgerigars left?' asked Mr Dempster, by way of distraction.

'The captain still has some,' volunteered Mr Akers as he put down a final entry into his notebook. 'And one native cat.'

'None of my birds survived,' said Mr Mayhew.

There were general nods of commiseration. Mr Sapsford had the most left of any of the passengers, which he attributed to his taking the advice given to him by Mr Berkeley to ensure they were always in the highest of the cages.

'Not everyone can have the highest cages, however, Mr Sapsford, can they?' asked Henrietta. She had one last parrot that had survived the journey—her favourite—the rainbow lorikeet.

'Looking forward to arriving, Lady Wood?' said Mr Akers.

Henrietta smiled but couldn't assemble a simple answer.

Mr Mayhew glanced at her in understanding. 'Lady Wood and I were reminiscing yesterday about our arrivals into Sydney.'

All the passengers had their tales.

Mrs Berkeley recalled her distress at the number of convicts when they passed through Hobart Town on their way to Sydney. 'But it's all changing, thank goodness—except the emancipists are still there, of course.'

Mr Mayhew said, 'I was so taken aback when I arrived in the colony. Somehow I'd imagined the lush vegetation of Jamaica and, instead, everything was so dry. It felt as if you touched a leaf it would crumble apart. I'd heard from Alfred Ferris that there was a drought on, but nothing prepares you for what that looks like and feels like. The Tank Stream was an open sewer with nothing running through to flush it out. Busby Bore was providing only a trickle of drinking water.'

With a show of deference, Mrs Sapsford bowed her head in Henrietta's direction. 'But Lady Wood probably has the best memories of the early days of the colony, so long ago, as a daughter of one of the first free settlers.'

Henrietta ignored the implied jibe at her age. 'I was six years old when I arrived in Sydney town with my family, but I remember some of it very well indeed. There can't have been a drought, because the streams that ran into the Parramatta River were full—so full, we had trouble fording them. I sat on my father's lap in the gig. Each time we crossed a creek, the water came up higher and higher—and then we were up the bank and trotting along the track.' She smiled with the recollection.

She felt the reassuring warmth of her father's arms, saw his broad hands holding the reins, heard the sounds of the whip birds piercing the chill damp air, felt the splashes as the gig ploughed through the rushing flow of water.

'Well, I don't think we'll have too many creeks to cross in London,' said Mr Berkeley, rising.

As if this were the signal, the passengers began to say their goodnights, and there were many farewells in case of missing the opportunity for those who were scheduled to leave in the morning.

Mr Mayhew stayed seated.

'You will stay in touch, won't you?' Henrietta asked.

'Yes, yes, of course. And may I introduce Lucy to you? I know you'd like her.'

'I'm sure I shall. And I shall be sure to tell her she must keep painting, even when her boorish husband wants her to be keeping house.'

He laughed and, taking a deep breath, said, 'Might you, I'm sure Lucy would, what I mean to say is, I would greatly appreciate it, if you might consider coming to our wedding?' For a moment, he looked as hesitant as he had been at the start of the voyage.

'Certainly, and Lucy shall have my rainbow lorikeet as a wedding present. That will be just the thing.'

The morning had been a scene of frantic activity as Mr Mayhew, the Berkeleys, Lieutenant Gordon and, unexpectedly, Mr Dempster left the ship at Folkestone. Their travelling luggage was lowered over to the pilot boat, leaving the rest to be collected from St Katherine Dock. After their departure, the ship felt empty, and Henrietta had spent most of the afternoon supervising Hill's final preparations for their own departure the following day.

Having managed to escape a teary Miss McPhail, Henrietta found herself alone on the deck in the deepening twilight. The summer air stroked her skin as the ship moved slowly on.

She could see the land alongside quite easily as they drew closer to London. At first there were only one or two pinpoints of light from the occasional cottage, and then a few clusters of lamp-lit windows grouped in ragged assembly as village after village went by.

As the sky began to deepen into a rich purple-blue, she could no longer see the shape of the land, and she lost the sense of it being the ship itself, which was moving. The banks were becoming covered with buildings, and more gas streetlamps sprang into life.

The reflections on the rippling surface of the water reminded her of the shine of the blue jellyfish creatures—she must remember to check that Hill had properly sealed the jar of her remaining specimen.

It was as if the lights were multiplying and gathering in twinkling streams, and parting, only to converge once more. They were like fireflies, she thought, blinking on and off and constantly moving.

And she was fourteen again, unable to sleep and standing on the deck wrapped in the balmy night air as the budgerow drew closer to Calcutta and the fireflies were fairies dancing to welcome her to her new life.

At that time she had known nothing of what awaited her, yet excitement had filled her. She knew as little of England; this country she called 'home'. For the first time in a long time, her heart quickened with that very same thrill; the thrill of not knowing what lay ahead.

THE END

Afterword

Lady Henrietta Wood kept in touch with Mr Morgan Mayhew after they arrived in England, and so continued to appear in his journal entries. On arrival, she went to stay with her brother-in-law, editor of the prominent magazine, *Bell's Life*, in London, in Norfolk Street, The Strand. She talked excitedly to Morgan of meeting the wife of Charles Dickens. She met up with Morgan and Lucy for sightseeing at the Tower of London and was a guest at their wedding.

Henrietta didn't succeed in her petition to obtain a full widow's pension, but she made do successfully on her part-pension. She travelled to and from England, India and Australia frequently—always first class. On one occasion, she had the adventure of being shipwrecked to add to her stories.

Her last visit to Australia was in early 1873.

Morgan's diary of that year recorded she visited him in Bathurst, New South Wales, where he was a Magistrate. His diary reported frequent dinners and calls during February. She would have been 73 years old and Morgan 54 years old.

When she returned to England that year, she wrote her memoirs, deftly excising any mention of her affair with de Bougainville.

Baron Hyacinthe de Bougainville wrote in his private journal that he had only fallen in love twice in his life, both times in Sydney. The first time was as a young man on the Baudin expedition, and the second time was in his forties, when he met Henrietta. He died the year before this voyage, at the end of an illustrious career.

Mr Morgan Mayhew married Lucy Butler in January the following year. Their only son was born during their voyage back to Sydney, somewhere near Heard Island in the southern Indian Ocean. Lucy was an acknowledged landscape and buildings painter, particularly active during the 1850s and 1860s, using charcoal or monochrome washes. Both Morgan and Lucy died in 1891. The connections between the Mayhew and Wood families continued over many generations, with Henrietta's stepson marrying Lucy's sister Amelia.

We don't know what happened in Lieutenant Gordon's life, but Mr Dempster and Morgan kept in touch during the year after arrival. Mr Dempster took lodgings in The Strand. He didn't marry Miss McPhail, however.

Later that year, Morgan records that Mr Dempster had told him that Miss McPhail had jilted him—writing a letter, begging to put an end to their engagement. Morgan omits to tell us Mr Dempster's reaction.

Morgan noted in his diary that he and Mr Dempster called on each other, dined together, played billiards and went to the opera to hear Jenny Lind in Roberto il Diavolo, so we can assume Mr Dempster was not too heartbroken.

Author's note

I have drawn heavily from available historical records to paint a picture of the lives of the main characters in this novel. I have retained the names of well-known historical figures who appear or who are referred to in the novel, and for whom considerable material is available upon which to ground their depiction. I have fictionalised the names of the main characters because I cannot know their personal feelings and motivations, and so the novel's plot, events and themes are my own invention. Thus, the Burbridge families and their relatives by birth or marriage are fictional characters, inspired by the family of Mr John Blaxland (older brother to the explorer, Gregory Blaxland). The character of Mr Morgan Mayhew is inspired by the lively diarist, Mr James Milbourne Marsh, whose journal entries informed a great many of the events in this novel. However, the story it tells of the secret letters and their passage from Sydney Harbour to somewhere in the North Atlantic Ocean is entirely a product of my imagination.

This novel is set shortly before the discovery of gold would radically alter the colony, with an influx of free settlers and capital. Even before the gold rush, however, the colony had begun to move away from its convict past, as the pastoral industries grew. The wider population was rapidly growing, so social connections were continually changing and adjusting. One of the areas of difficulty in writing this novel was in reconciling the views of the historical characters about race and class with contemporary cultural awareness.

The historical characters of this novel lived among a small elite (the 'exclusives') within a penal colony. The main source of labour for their homes and estates was provided by convicts, convicts' children, and convicts who had served their time ('emancipists'). The emancipists thrived on the business opportunities in the new colony, with many becoming as rich or richer than their former masters. The class sensibilities of the free elite therefore were necessarily pragmatically blind where business was concerned, though it was still acute in social situations.

The settlement sat at the edge of a large continent populated by multiple Aboriginal tribes whose clan groups were being progressively dispossessed with the uptake of land as the colony grew. The contact between European settlers and Indigenous peoples was at its most direct and most conflicted in areas of new occupation. The attitudes described in this novel were based on family records and were typical of people of their class. Awareness of Aboriginal people was strikingly absent in the personal records from the time period.

For a detailed bibliography of sources and a detailed bibliography of sources and a longer factual account of the events and people who inspired this work of fiction, readers may be interested in the short biography I have written previously on the life of Harriet Blaxland.

A Ferguson, *A gentleman's daughter: The life of Harriet Mary Dowling (nee Blaxland) in India and Australia in colonial times*, Backstory Press, New South Wales, 2017.

(available in e-book or paperback via Amazon)

Acknowledgements

My thanks again to my husband, Ian King. Without his detailed background knowledge of the Blaxland history and his constant support and encouragement, this project would have stalled a long time ago. My thanks are also owed to Richard Blaxland and Wendy Blaxland for their enthusiastic support. I am very appreciative of the librarians at the State Library of New South Wales for enabling my access to their collection which includes materials related to the Blaxland, Dowling and Walker families.

Many thanks are also owed to Michael Heath-Caldwell, Peter Dowling, and Keith Harrison for their time and generosity in sharing information about James Milbourne Marsh. My thanks too to the helpful librarian at the Society of Australian Genealogists in Sydney (for the opportunity to view the original diary of James Augustus Milbourne Marsh). The copyright for his diaries and letters is held by Keith Harrison who kindly granted permission for me to make use of this material in this work of fiction.

My thanks to the members of the Lake Macquarie branch of the Fellowship of Australian Writing for their support and invaluable feedback in the development of this novel and my other writing over many years. Thanks also to my trusty beta-readers—Jenny Ferneyhough, Sue McAllister, and Glenys Murray—for their insightful comments and suggestions on this story and all the others. And finally, thanks too for the polish to the final product from the detailed editing provided courtesy of the Manuscript Appraisal Agency. Any remaining glitches remain, of course, my own.

About the author

After completing a degree in writing in the early 70s, my interest in communication led me to qualify and work as a speech pathologist in clinical and academic settings. Now retired, I am pursuing my long-standing fascination with story writing across diverse genres.

In 2017, I self-published 'A Gentleman's Daughter'—a biography of Harriet Blaxland (later, Lady Dowling) who lived a colourful life in colonial New South Wales and India (available in paperback and eBook through Amazon and other online retailers). Over the last few years, I have written a number of award-winning short stories ranging across crime, horror, and historical science fiction. My unpublished science-fiction novel 'Grey Nomad' was shortlisted for the 2019 Fantastic Prize (Brio Books), the Queensland Writers' Centre 2020 Adaptable and Publishable programs, and I currently have a crime novel 'in the works'.

The Sisters' Saga

Henrietta's sisters collect flowers to catalogue and make detailed drawings. But Henrietta is not like them. She lets the petals scatter where they may. Set in colonial Sydney and Calcutta in the early 1800s, *The Sisters' Saga* is a historical fiction trilogy which tells of three sisters and the compromises they must make to reconcile love's delusions with the demands of reality.

Maiden Manoeuvres is a coming of age story, following the wilful eldest sister, Henrietta Burbridge, in the early 1800s in colonial Sydney and her impetuous marriage at 16 years-of-age in Calcutta.

In *Dearest Daughter*, the lives of the younger sisters, Rose and Beth Burbridge are turned upside down by Henrietta's return from India. Now back in colonial Sydney between 1825-35, Henrietta asks why, if matrimony is the bedrock of the families, is it so hard for love to survive marriage? But her sisters must answer a very different question: How much would they trade for matrimony?

The events of *Widow's Wake* take place in 1847 over the course of a single voyage as Henrietta leaves Sydney to return to London. Widowed for the second time, Henrietta struggles to reconcile the regrets of her past in order to embrace the adventures ahead. She is the heroine of the colourful tales she shares with young Mr Morgan Mayhew. However, their 1847 voyage from Sydney to London will be one tale neither will ever divulge.

Companion volume:

Ferguson, A. (2017). *A gentleman's daughter: The life of Henrietta Mary Wood (nee Burbridge) in India and Australia in colonial times.* Newcastle, NSW: Backstory Press (available in e-book or paperback via Amazon).